The ELEMENTAL Wars

Liv
Elizabeth
Clark

The Elemental Wars: Mist
Liv Elizabeth Clark

Cover art by
Lindsey Clark-Burton

This book is a work of fiction. Names, characters, places, and incidents are the product of the author's imagination or are used fictitiously. Any resemblance to actual events, locales, or persons, living or deceased, is coincidental.

ISBN: 979-8-218-42836-5

<u>for</u>
my parents, Jackie and Steven

my hands, my guides, my supporters,
and the people who put up with all of my shenanigans

I love you more than anything. thank you for everything you've done
for me and this dream of mine

Prologue 3029

Murder is fun. Murder makes the world go round. Everyone has at some point or another dreamt of killing someone. But almost nobody has killed someone while dreaming–or something of the sorts.

So, a long, long, long, long, longlonglonglong time ago, these giant *creatures* decided to murder a bunch of people. Screams. Horror. Blood. Ahh! Yeah, it was gruesome. Or so I've heard. And seen, though I hadn't exactly been born at the time–but we're not there yet. Yet. I said yet.

These things were, like, literally the most deadly things the world has ever seen besides Will Smith's iconic slap at the Oscars in 2022. They were huge and violent and very very scary. Very scary. Trust me. Picture the most ugly, horrifying thing you could ever imagine. Now multiply it by that one mouth breather you know.

They had to be trapped.

Sent away.

Caged.

Confined.

And I know what it's like to be caged. It sucks. It's hard. Knowing that there is such a large world out there and not being able to ever see it. The urge to escape is like a beast clawing at your windpipe and trying–*begging*–to get out. Well, more specifically, to get *you* out.

And these creatures experienced that. That sensation. One in particular experienced it a lot worse. It fought. It fought harder than you'd think possible. This demon thing wanted out. It didn't like being caged. And after a while, it worked. It broke free.

So, as a result, the people of this world *had* to find a solution. To try to put the creature back in with the others would let them all come tumbling out, but to leave it as is, would cost millions their lives. Soooooooo, they found...another solution.

The creature was placed and sealed in a living vessel. A human girl.

That was a while ago. She is no longer living. But the creature still has a vessel. It's not like they are roaming free, lurking in shadows and awaiting the moment when they can strike. No.

It's trapped inside someone else. And that person is trapped inside a prison. The largest prison in Bludriss. The LEFP. The best prison there is. At least, that's what they claim–the prison workers, not the vessel. The vessel hates it there. They were sent there when they were little, which isn't abnormal since the LEFP gets tons of kids–all dangerous. But the vessel hadn't done anything. They did nothing wrong. There was no real reason for them to be sent to such a place. Especially since they were never even informed of being a vessel until they were, like, basically fifteen.

And it makes me so angry. It makes me feel so alone.

I didn't do anything. So why the hell am I here?

red and blue
the sirens
so loud, so bright
their sounds cry out,
piercing the night
the bulbs on the top give out a blinding light
they break down the door
no sympathy in sight
i turn them black and blue
though i was told not to fight
then the sirens disappear and my eyes lose sight

i will get revenge
no matter how hard you try
i will get revenge
in the midst of the night

red and blue
the colors still cause me fright

–PRISONER JOURNAL OF
SUBJECT 3029

first 3029

I don't remember how old I was. But it was one of my oldest memories. Something that I'd thought about all the time for almost all of my life. It was the memory that shaped my core and my beliefs. The memory that shook my world. It was also the memory that completely changed who I was. For the worse.

● ● ●

The lights were off. It was somewhere between the hours of dusk and dawn so it was dark out. Who needs the lights anyway? Things are already bright enough.

I was laying in my small room. The walls were colorless. They were like an unfinished basement or a garage. Dry-wall framed the room. The floors were dark brown wood. Each slice of flooring was a different length. My bed was a small blow-up mattress that I barely fit on. The sheet of cloth on top of it was what was supposed to be my blanket. It was a dirty off-white color and was fraying at the edges. My pillow was an old sack of dried beans that my mother had reluctantly given me. They kind of smelled if I was being honest. But, by now, I was so used to it. It no longer bothered me. There was nothing else in the room besides me and my book.

The book I was reading had a blue-ish cover with golden letters on the front. *Peter Pan,* I believe it was called. It had treasures inside that I couldn't even dream of.

I was wearing the same thing I always was. My father's old work T-shirt that went a long way past my waist, my black glove that only covered my wrist, my palm, and the back of my hand; and my underwear. My hair ran a little past my shoulders and was lying down. Except for the large braid that was on the left side of my head.

My door was locked from the outside. That's how it always was.

Honestly, I was fine with my life. Though my parents avoided me, I still got food and my own room and I wasn't abused or anything of the sorts. I truly believed that, deep down, my parents were good people. Even if they paid little to no attention to my existence.

The small town we lived in was peaceful and there wasn't usually any crime. So it surprised me when I heard sirens. They were loud and stabbed my eardrums. I dropped the book I was holding and covered the sides of my head. They gradually got louder until my entire room turned red and blue. I couldn't even hear my own thoughts. I squeezed my eyelids shut, but darkness wasn't what I saw. The lights were bright enough to light up my vision even if I couldn't see.

I waited for the sounds to pass, but they didn't. A few moments later, there was a loud banging on the front door. Chatter overlapped with footsteps heading for the door and a creak as it was opened. My stomach tightened, nervousness clawing at my insides.

The doorknob on the door to my room shook and keys rattled beyond the hinged barrier. When it opened, my mother and father stepped aside and seven armed men filed in. They all had identical body attire: navy-blue helmets with yellow-tinged visors; dark blue uniform shirts with countless pockets, a badge and a name tag; and matching pants and boots. They were equipped with shields and black batons.

"Xandralin Raq, you are now going under custody of the LEFP. You can come peacefully or forcefully. Your choice," the man in front boomed.

My heart picked up pace and sweat ran down my back. They were here for me. Confusion and fear froze over my mind.

"Xan," my mother pleaded, her voice teary, "please go peacefully."

The LEFP? Lunatic...Encagement...Facility...Prison...?

"You...you're sending me...to the LEFP?" I whispered. I stood up, my heart aching and my breathing coming in harsher gasps. I didn't know what I was doing. My legs were just kind of moving. It happened without me being completely aware of it.

"Don't make this more complicated than it needs to be," one of the men told me. I'm pretty sure that the thing that pushed me off the deep end was when I realized that my parents had sold me out. I lost all sense of reality. I couldn't see or hear anything. I was plunged into darkness and felt no sensation from my limbs.

Occasionally, I heard grunts and sometimes gasps of pain and felt something hit my clenched knuckles. I wasn't able to determine what was going on. I felt trapped inside of my own head. Panic spread throughout me. What was happening?

Eventually, everything came back to me. I could see everything around me, though it was mostly just the floor. I could feel everything once again, as well. My hands were cuffed behind my back and I was pinned to the ground. Multiple men were on the ground, bruised and beaten up. My eyes started filling with a hot liquid.

"…!" I couldn't get myself to speak the words that flooded through my brain. *Did…did I do that to them?*

My parents were standing in the doorway. Their faces were filled with terror. Hot, painstakingly obvious, terror. But…why?

"Miss. Raq, we have been given permission by your legal guardians to take you into custody." The man who spoke paused. "*For life.*"

"…?!"

Before I could react, something hard hit my head. And the world went dark.

alone
it causes eternal suffering
you cannot reverse
it pushes you down
and puts you against the universe
this terrible place draws out its own curse
only the people who live in this horror
know the troubles that are in for us

what do i do if it's here i grow old?
but one day my power will be released
and i shall go bold
i am a person for which prison cannot hold

–PRISONER JOURNAL OF

SUBJECT 3029

Second   5742

The first time I saw her was in the cafeteria. I was sitting with my one and only friend.

"Jaymon," I said as I tugged on his sleeve to get his nose out of his stupid book. He looked up at me.

"What?" he snapped, visibly annoyed.

"Look." He followed my extended finger to the doorway where *five guards* were bringing in a girl who looked to be around my age. Five guards!

"No," Jay told me, opening his book again.

"No...*what?*"

"You want to be friends with her."

"What's so bad about that?"

"Rowan, I'm not becoming friends with a girl."

"I know you don't get along with many people, but–" He cut me off.

"*Many?* You're my only friend."

"Whatever. Anyway, I was pointing out how dangerous she must be. Heck, I only got two Guards! When you first came you had, what? Three? She's got *five!* Man, she must'a killed a lot!"

"You drowned your parents. I know. But not everyone gets into the

LEFP for killing," Jaymon lectured. I put my elbow on the table and used the heel of my hand to hold my face up.

"Blah, blah, blah." He rolled his eyes at me.

Then the unexpected happened.

The man walking at the front of the group opened his mouth and called out in a deep voice, "Jaymon Rivereay, Rowan Samrish. Where are thee?" My hand shot up. Beside me, Jay raised his hand slightly, all the while continuing to read.

"STAND!" My chair squeaked as I shot up. I wasn't very scared of guards. I was more of a laid-back sorta person. But this guard was...different.

Jaymon sighed, set his book down on the table, and stood up. The whole room had gone completely silent. The *entire cafeteria*. That did *not* ease my nerves. The guard walked over to us with the other four and the girl following close behind.

"This is subject 3029. She shall eat breakfast here. Guards are watching for suspicious behavior in her, but thou shalt get her to talk about markings." He grabbed her arm, swung her forward, and let her crash into the table. It rocked and Jay's water tipped and spilled. He twitched when it got close to his book.

"Good luck." Then he and his loyal followers left us.

"The heck?" I asked aloud, watching them retreat.

"I'm sorry," came a fragile female voice.

"...?" I turned around and the girl was wiping up the water with the sleeve of her shirt. I took the opportunity to study her.

She was wearing the same outfit we were: white button-down, long-sleeved shirt; black pants, and no shoes or socks. She had straight black hair that ran a little past her shoulders. There was a large braid on the left side of her head. She had freckles on her cheeks and light purple eyes that were framed with heavy eyelashes. But most importantly and distinctively, her left hand had a black glove on it that went a bit past her wrist and had open fingers. Her fingers had weird colored lines on them. Her middle finger had light blue lines and her other fingers had dark blue lines.

I sat down just as she touched the tip of the chair in front of me and then retracted her hand.

"Do you guys mind if I...?" she asked.

"Not really," I responded when Jaymon didn't. She pulled back the dark green chair and took a seat. The number on the left side of her neck read: 3029.

"My name's Rowan Samrish, nice to meet you," I said to her. I wanted to stick out my hand for her to shake it, but a tiny voice in the back of my head told me that I shouldn't. That she wouldn't take it. So I kept my hands to myself.

Beside me, Jay reluctantly added his own name to the introductions.

"Jaymon Rivereay." He didn't even look at her. *Cooold.*

"I'm Xandralin Raq. I kind of prefer to go by 'Xan', though. I like it a bit better," she responded, her voice fading.

"Cool."

Xan stared into her lap for a few minutes before Jay sighed, shut his book audibly, and crossed his arms across his chest.

"Aren't you going to eat?" he asked her, clearly annoyed by something.

"I-I'm not hungry."

"Okay, fine. Markings. Let's talk about those." He was cutting to the chase. Not wasting time. He was trying to do what the guard had instructed us to do. Though, the suggested topic was quickly turned down.

"Let's not," she responded immediately. Jaymon's eyes narrowed. His left eye was covered by his dark brown hair.

"How old are you?"

"Eight."

"What's an 8-year-old doing with a tattoo?" Xan stiffened. I elbowed him, whispering for him to quit, but I couldn't deny that I was also curious. But curiosity killed the cat.

"I don't want to talk about it."

"Fine."

"So, Xan," I piped, "I wanna know, what'd you do to end up in the LEFP?"

"Nothing."

"...Huh?" Jay and I asked together.

"I didn't do anything. That's the truth of it. What about you guys?"

I let that sink in. "Wait, wait, wait. You're telling me that you got put into the Lunatic Encagement Facility Prison, had five guards escort you to the cafeteria, and had to be put into a group that they could spot, and you didn't even do anything to make that happen?!"

"Correct."

"Dang, girl!" Jay stared at me in utter disbelief that I would actually say that out loud.

"Now, us. Well, I did things that are none of your business. Rowan, your turn." *Well...okay.* Jay had never said what he did so it was typical that he would say something like that.

"I drowned both my parents." I plugged in false emotion to make it sound like I didn't care.

"Wow," Xan exclaimed.

She paused for a second. "Hey, Rowan, Jaymon?"

"Yeah?" I asked.

"...?" Jay looked up at her.

"What're these?" She pulled down the collar of her shirt and pointed to the numbers that were tattooed onto her neck.

"That's your subject number," Jay explained.

"...Sub...ject number?"

"Everyone has one. They use those to figure out who everyone is rather than using our names all the time." He pointed to his own. "See? I'm 1863. And Rowan is 5742."

"Interesting."

"It's also your cell-ish number," I added.

"Cell...-ish?"

"Yeah. It's a little more like a room than a prison cell."

"Okay. Good to know."

The bell rang. It wasn't that loud, but Xan jumped and covered her ears with her hands. She started shaking slightly like she was afraid of it.

"It's okay," I said. "It's just the bell. It just means that we're dismissed from breakfast. Let's go to my room."

"Rowan–"

"Oh, c'mon, Jay. It'll be fine." He didn't seem happy about it, but he went along with it and didn't argue further.

So we went up to my room and chatted for a few hours. Then, after a bit, something no one expected happened. Xan became closer to Jay and I than we were to each other.

I still don't understand these stupid journals.
I mean, I've been here for over seven years
now and nothing has happened. My only
friends are still Jay and Xan. I'm still bored
out of my mind! And I'm still trying to forget.
But it isn't going away. I'm still having
nightmares and being watched by the guards.
I hope to one day get out of here.
That's all I've ever really wanted.

-PRISONER JOURNAL OF

SUBJECT 5742

third 3029

I had earplugs in, but I still heard the bell. I sat up, caught off-guard. My hands automatically covered my head, trying to block out the noise. When it stopped, I looked around my 'cell-ish' as Rowan calls it.

It had light brown walls with a barred window beside my bed. My bed was a couple of feet off the ground, supported by a metal frame. It had a spring mattress that fit my whole body and a quilt and actual pillow. The flooring was the same as my old room. The left wall held two doors. One was a small personal bathroom and the other led outside. The outside door was guarded by a young man. Each prisoner was assigned someone. They stood outside the subject's door and carefully watched whoever went in or came out. The only other items in the room were a desk, a stool, a pencil, my journal, a small book, and a picture frame that I had face down on the desk.

I got up and opened the door to the bathroom and stared at my reflection in the small circular mirror. The girl who stared back at me had black hair that ran a bit past her shoulders. Freckles dotted the space under her violet eyes.

I undid my braid and then placed the hair tie on the sink and picked up the wooden hairbrush. I stroked my hair and let my mind's gears grind into motion.

Right. Today's his birthday. That means it isn't long before it's mine.

I separated the top half of the left side of my hair into three strands and then started weaving. Once I was done, I stared at my reflection again.

Banging erupted in my ears.

"3029, are you up? The bell has already rang!"

I sighed and then ran out, flipping the lights off. When I flung open the door, I felt it slam into something.

"*Ahk!*"

I closed it. Then leaned down to face the person in front of me. "Yes, Lijin, I'm awake." He was sitting on the floor with his nose cupped in his hands that leaked a red liquid. He had on the standard uniform for guards, but he didn't have the helmet. He just had a dark blue baseball cap with the LEFP's logo on it—the acronym of the title locked behind bars. He stared up at me. When Lijin spoke, his voice was weird and sounded like he was plugging his nose.

"Man, you're worse than the serial killers." I smiled and held up my index and middle fingers.

"Accomplishment!" I giggled. "Well, I'm off to the cafeteria. Seeya!" I skipped away. I went a couple paces down the right side of the hallway until I reached the stairs. I took them three steps at a time, humming a random tune all the while. Floor 2. Floor 1. Ground Level. My bare feet hit the smooth floor. The heavy doors were open with several guards watching everyone like hawks. I ignored them, skipping by like they weren't even there.

"*Xan!*" I turned to the small table off to the side that was screeching my name. Sitting at the table were two boys who were just a bit older than me. One of them had dark brown hair that covered his left eye. His right eye was a bright hazel. Nose in a book, he was very calm and composed, but had a very fast and effective mind. The other boy had orange-ish-red hair. He had light brown eyes that were very good at spotting things quickly. He was the other boy's opposite with a bubbly attitude and boisterous tone. He was the one flagging me down.

"Hey, guys!" I said as I trotted over to them.

"Sup," Book-Worm said. He had a new book in hand.

"Another new one? Where do you get them from, Jay?" Jaymon Rivereay. Reason for imprisonment: unknown.

"He bribes his guard," the red-head told me. Rowan Samrish. Reason for imprisonment: drowned parents.

I sat down. I noticed Jay staring at me. I rolled my eyes. *I didn't forget, nitwit.*

"Uh, guys?" Rowan asked. I lifted my first three fingers just high enough that Jay could see them and then counted down. When my index finger retracted into my palm, we both took a heavy breath in.

"Happy 16th birthday, Rowan!!" we exclaimed as we both pulled out cards made from scrap paper out of our pants' pockets. He read them both in the matter of seconds.

"Thanks, you guys," he said.

"Now," I clapped my hands together, "what do you want for breakfast? But it has to be on our menu." Rowan laughed.

"You don't get a choice. You eat what they serve, idiot."

"Great choice!" I exclaimed. Jay chuckled quietly at my, uh, ... questionable... attempt at hostility. "C'mon." I stood up and waved them to the "lunch" line. It was more of a 'breakfast line' at this time of day, but 'lunch line' sounds better. Both boys stood up and followed me.

One thing that I learned in my seven years at the LEFP is that everyone knows something about myself that I was never told. I asked Lijin, but he brushed it off. I'm sure it has to do with my hand, but 'why' is not something I know. Everyone looks at me weird and cowers when I get close. I think they're scared of me. But...why? I was fourteen and most of the prisoners were older men.

As we passed a table of five grown men I heard one of them whisper to the rest, "Look. It's 3029. She kills everythin' in sight. She ain't got no friends 'cept those two scumbags. Stay away from her. I'll tell ya, she's–" Jay punched him, knocking his head to the side, spit flinging from his mouth.

"Shut up!" he growled. " 'Cause the scumbags kill, too! Don't act like you're safe! Or quiet, matter of fact."

"Thanks, Jay," I whispered to him.

"No, prob."

A scrawny guard ran up to us and put out his hand like he was pushing something backwards. "1863, I have been ordered to stand by you for fifteen minutes hence your previous actions." Jay blinked then shrugged his shoulders and walked around him.

"Whatever."

We hopped in line and grabbed our trays. I didn't even bother to look at what it was. When we sat back down the guard had already given up and retreated.

"Geez, this place is tight. Punch a guy for being a moron and you get birded," Rowan complained as he shoved a plastic spoon full of...something that might have been soup...into his mouth. I sucked on an orange juice box that had honestly probably expired, like, four months ago. "You notice this now?"

"Took him long enough." Jaymon was picking at his something-berries.

"It's not like I just noticed that. I mean, I hit that stupid Kilo guy and then Taku was on my case for a freaking month." Taku was Rowan's personal guard. He was quite a bit older than mine so Rowan couldn't smash his face with a door like I could to Lijin.

"Mine acts like he cares, but he's too much of a coward to actually do something. He said he'd watch me for fifteen minutes. Nine minutes later and he's already scurrying back to his post." He eyed the back corner where the small man was standing.

"Lijin doesn't punish me for anything. I broke his nose this morning and he didn't do anything about it. Just sat there."

"Well he's still considered new, isn't he? He probably still just doesn't realize that you aren't actually allowed to kill him if he sets you straight." Rowan made faces at his spoon when he realized that he had completely missed his mouth.

"Whatever." I waved my hand. "Let's drop it. So...what are we going to do for Rowan's birthday?"

"We don't have to do any–" I put my finger to his mouth.

"Shhh...Your opinion doesn't matter. I was talking to Jay." He laughed.

"Let's hang out in your room," Jaymon suggested. My insides squeezed.

My room?

"Ooh, yeah! C'mon, Xan! We haven't seen your room in ages!"

"It looks like a room," I told him.

"Yeah, well how would I know? I've never seen it." I sighed. Took them long enough to get persistent. It'd been years since we'd been in it together. But it was Rowan's birthday. And this was what he wanted to do.

"I guess," I caved. The bell rang.

"*Ahk!*" I pressed my palms to my ears, my head threatening to explode. The sound echoed painfully inside my skull. Seven years had gone by and I still hadn't gotten used to it.

When the interruption stopped I let my hands fall into my lap. We sighed in sync. Then, picking up our trays and pushing out our chairs, we emptied what little food was left and then headed out the doors. We ran through the hallway and then bounded up the stairs. Floor 1. Floor 2. Floor 3. I stopped once we reached the bronze door with the numbers 3029 on it. Lijin was not yet here. Probably still in the cafeteria.

"Right here," I said, even if it was kinda obvious. Then I opened the door. I suspected that they were shocked that it was so empty. Because all a prisoner had was their most important belongings and...well...I had very little of those.

Sure enough, Rowan whispered, "I-it's so...empty."

"Yeah," Jay agreed.

"That's all I had." I led them inside. I don't think they'd ever really sat down and looked at everything that I kept in here. And, well, clearly, that's because there wasn't much to look at. Jay tenderly caressed the book that laid on the bed.

"I don't think I've ever seen you read."

"Are these..." came a small voice from Rowan, "your parents?"

"...!" I spun around with a start. The wooden frame was wedged between Rowan's pale fingers. He was staring intently at the photograph. "Hey!" I yelled and snatched the stupid frame from him. My bare hand slammed it face down back onto the desk. His irises shrank, startled.

"Sorry...You see, I meant to decline when they offered it, but I j-just can't bring myself to hate them enough to not accept the photo. So I keep it face down on my desk."

"Makes sense...I-I guess," muttered Rowan.

"They sold me out...But they raised me."

"S-sold you out?" Jay questioned, confused. My left hand twitched uncontrollably, the blood flow that led to my fingers growing cold until I shoved it behind my back and smiled at them.

"It's nothing to fold over for. Just my stupid past. Let it be, okay?" They nodded. "Alright. What do we want to do?" Jay set his book down beside my journal. He stared at the cover that said Xandralin A. Raq - 3029. His face lost composure and crumpled in what looked like pain. I tapped his shoulder and his features shifted back to normal. He stepped away and fell down on the bed, sighing.

"We could tease the guard," Rowan suggested.

"That's always fun. Sure!" Jay rolled his eyes at me. "Stop judging me!!" I whined like a child.

"Yeah, Jay, that's not nice."

"Oh, can it."

"Let's camp here and figure out how to get Lijin put in his place. He is most likely on his way here so it won't give us very long," I told them. Both boys nodded. I gave us around five to ten minutes before Lijin could return to the outside of my door. My childish side took over. We could push him down stairs...No...He might actually die. What about dropping my book from the ceiling?...How in the world am I supposed to get up there? I guess we could–

The door swung open. "Xan! I-I mean 3029, I–er–you need to come with me!" Lijin yelled, snapping me and my friends out of our sinister plotting.

"What?! Why?!"

"..." He didn't respond.

"Lijin?"

"Just come on." He grabbed my wrist. Then he pulled me out the door, leaving Jay and Rowan to ponder what was going on.

seven years
they're what causes me to lose my mind
and go insane
i try to count the years
but i've lost track of all the days
washed away by my tears
is all my numbed pain
i can't tell you how many times
i thought it would go away
instead of jovial sunshine
there is only rain
i shall never feel without loneliness again
until i've completely lost all sanity
will my inevitable self remain

–PRISONER JOURNAL OF

SUBJECT 3029

fourth 7560

She was clearly very confused. I mean, who wouldn't be? I had just torn her from her room with no explanation. But she probably wouldn't have come with me if I had given a reason for my actions.

She tried to pull her wrist free, but I held on.

"Lijin, what is going on?!" she cried, frustrated. I kept walking towards Ground Level. My orders swarmed in my head.

Bring her to the telephone visitation room. They want to talk to her...Bring her to the telephone visitation room. They want to talk to her...Bring–

"TERAKI!"

"*Ahhg*!" I jumped. "What?!"

"I'm not taking a blind road."

"...?" I sighed, then let go of her wrist. We had made it to the stairs that led to Floor 1. *So close.*

"You have visitors."

"...?" Xan thought that over. "Well, I don't know anybody besides..." It was visible when it hit her who she was seeing. Her eyes filled with fury. "NO!!" she screamed.

"Xan, c'mon–"

"I am *not* talking to them!"

"Please. They really want to talk to you."

"About what, huh? How they ghosted me for seven years?" She crossed her arms and puffed out her cheeks like a toddler.

"Listen, I don't know what went through their heads when they pretended you didn't exist. But, they're back now and I think you should hear them out." Her features scrunched up, deep in thought.

"...Fine," she said, succumbing to my request.

"Good." I took her wrist–a little less forcefully this time–and started walking down the metal stairs. "Just try to be nice...-ish?"

"Nice-ish? Yeesh. That's a hard thing to live up to," Xan responded. I couldn't tell if it was sarcasm or not. She stared at the ground, watching her footing as we walked. Her black hair bounced ever so slightly as we neared the end of the staircase. My eyes drifted to the hand held in mine. Her glove was still on her hand, but I could see the blue lines on her fingers. That stupid mark. The poor kid didn't even know what it meant.

"I can walk by myself. You don't have to lead me," the girl told me with distaste. I let go of her wrist, retracting my gloved hand to my chest.

"Oh, uh, right. Sorry." We rounded a corner and then began descending the stairs to Ground Level.

"Hey, uh, Lijin?" Xan whispered.

"...? What's up?"

"I'm leaving if they say it was for the better." I nodded slowly, understanding entirely.

We reached the stone floor and then headed for the telephone visitation room. My boots and her bare feet made footsteps that echoed throughout the hallway. The double doors came into view. I placed my hand on them and began to push them open when I realized that Xan wasn't moving. She just stood there, biting her lip with her upper front teeth. Her body shook violently as an obvious shiver ran through her. She took a step backward. Then another as she shook her head back and forth.

"I don't wanna go in."

I knew that I would come to regret the decision if I told her she didn't have to, so instead I said, "You've got to."

Her violet eyes were filled deep with a sudden overflow of ominous emotion. That threw me off and I stuttered in my next reply.

"Th-they missed y-you. H-hopefully they wish to apologize."

"I hope so."

I pushed the heavy iron doors open with both hands. The first thing I noticed was that there were several full-fledged guards. They were all staring at me with smug looks on their faces, as if to say, "Took him long enough." The next thing I noticed was the couple sitting at the table with two phones and glass separating the visitors from the prisoners. The woman of the two had a long black braid that draped over her right shoulder. I couldn't see her eyes because of the reflection in her glasses. She was wearing a professional suit and had her hands folded neatly atop the table. The man had short gray hair that spiked up in some places. His hazel eyes were filled with fear and expectation. Also wearing a suit, the man was awkwardly adjusting his tie. Then I noticed how composed Xan looked all of a sudden.

When the woman noticed her, she leaned forward slightly.

"Xan!" she cried.

"Mother, Father." She bowed to them.

"Mr. and Mrs. Raq," one of the higher-ranking guards boomed, "this is Sergeant Lijin Teraki. He is 3029's personal guard. He has been watching her for the past four years. Teraki, this is Abagail and Zach Raq, 3029's legal guardians." He didn't sound exactly thrilled.

I bowed and held back disgust for the couple. "Nice to meet you." Then, placing my hand on her back, I pushed Xan forward. She looked up at me and then turned to her parents and walked over to the small stool on the prisoner side of the table. She picked up the old-school phone and she was mirrored by the couple.

"Hello again," Xan said.

"Oh, Xan. It's been so long," Abagail sighed. "I almost didn't recognize you."

"Seven years. That's how long you completely forgot I existed."

"No, honey. We-we needed to stay away so that you could get used to your new life here," Zach tried to explain.

"Get used to it?! I was used to it three weeks in!!"

"Well...you know...it's clearly...still there...so we wanted to give it some time." Abagail looked down at the hand resting on the table. Xan yanked it backwards and then shoved it under to grip her pants tighter than the fabric should be able to endure.

"I don't even know what '*it*' is. You won't tell me. And it's my hand. Not yours. Leaving me to figure out life as an 8-year-old is not for my well-being! It's you guys being afraid of whatever my mark means!"

"Trust us. It was for the better."

"No, Father, it definitely wasn't!" She laughed as the bubbles of anger popped. I took a hesitant step forward and reached out my hand. But an arm raised and blocked my way.

"Stand down, Teraki."

"But–" I protested.

"She can't do anything to them. There's too many of us."

I thought about what she told me as we walked. *"I'm leaving if they say it was for the better."* They had said the exact sentence that she said would drive her out of the room, but she showed no sign of retreating. She must've had something that she wanted to say to them and was waiting for the right moment to do so.

"Give me a real reason," Xan demanded. "Why'd you abandon me?"

"We didn't abandon you." The woman's eyes narrowed behind her glasses.

"Then what do you call what you did?"

"We did the right thing."

"Oh, really?! Why did you come to see me?!"

"...We just wanted to see our daughter," the man murmured.

"I'm not your daughter anymore." She smiled. "I can fend for myself now. I mean, I've already been doing it for almost seven years. I'm fourteen now, retards." She extended her index and middle fingers, cocking her head slightly to the side. Then giggled.

Xan dropped the phone and then stood up and started to walk towards me and the door.

"Xandralin Amethyst, stop right there!!" Abagail screamed. She was loud enough that she didn't even need the phone.

"...?" Xan turned around slowly, groaning quietly, and taking her time with each degree.

"TAKE. THAT. BACK."

"No."

"Xandralin!"

"What?"

"You will always be our daughter! You can't change that!" My heart throbbed painfully.

"I'll be your daughter once you can look at me without fear."

"...!" Apparently, Abagail didn't think that Xan would be able to read her, though I was pretty sure everyone could.

"Honey, we aren't s-scared of you."

"Yeah," Zach countered. "Me and your mother hold no fear towards you."

"Well, in that case..." Xan walked over and stood atop of the stool. Her parents scrunched back.

"Hey, hey, hey!" a guard yelled.

"Hold up," I said. "Let's see what she does. You said it yourself; there's too many of us for something to seriously go wrong." *I hope.* They stared at me with questioning looks, but obeyed my commands anyway, falling back and leaving Xan alone. She reached over top of the glass, standing on one foot.

"Touch my hand," she ordered. They just stared at her in obviously terrified states. "Knew it." She hopped down and turned her attention to me. "I want to return to Rowan and Jay."

It took me a second to respond. "O-okay." She started to walk out the doors. I bowed to her guardians. "Thanks for coming." Their expressions told me that they remembered the same thing I did. So as everyone turned away, I faced them, smirking, and stuck up my middle finger. "Suckers."

● ● ●

We walked in silence until we reached the bottom of the stairs that led up to Floor 3. I got fed up with the quiet and tried to start a conversation.

"We weren't in there very long." I mentally slapped myself for being the world's worst conversation starter.

"They tick me off. I didn't want to be in there," Xan responded, her violet eyes fixed on the top of the stairs.

Tell me about it. I rolled my eyes along with my unspoken thoughts.

"What are you going to tell the boys?" I asked.

"My parents came to see me. They had to leave." She shrugged. "No big deal."

"...O-*kay.*"

"...Lijin?"

"Yeah?"

She looked straight ahead, not even glancing at me.

"I'm sorry...about your nose." I reached up and touched the bandage that covered the bridge of my nose. Soft pain jolted through my face. The prison nurse had stopped the bleeding and snapped it back into place a few minutes after Xan had deserted me in the hallway. But I had taken worse. Much worse. It was almost laughable.

"It's nothing," I replied, bringing my hand back down and waving it off. Then I eyed her suspiciously. She never apologized for anything. Not anymore. "Okay, what's the catch?"

"What?! A catch?!" She sounded deeply offended, but I saw through the act. "No! *But*...it would be nice if you didn't say anything since I apologized to you." Ah. So she wanted her reaction to her parents to be kept secret.

"Mmm...fine," I said, bending easily.

We turned into the hallway and soon reached her door. There was soft muttering coming from inside. *So the boys never left.* Xan sighed heavily and then her face masked every ounce of emotion that resulted from her meeting with her parents.

She opened the door. Her friends were sitting on the floor.

"Xan!" the red-head called.

"That was quick," the other boy muttered. "What'd they want you for?"

Xan waved her hand. "My parents came to visit, but they ended up having to go back to work," she lied fluently. Then she stepped into the room, turned around, and waved to me.

"Bye, Lijin!" Then her smile faltered and she mouthed, "Thank you."

"Bye," I whispered pathetically. The door closed with a slight creak. I flinched, though it wasn't loud.

Abagail and Zach Raq. The names drove me into my painful past. Blood. Knives. Tears. Love. Mourning. Salvation. Then the people that took all that was left.

I wanted to stand by Xan. To tell her everything that her parents kept hidden. But all she knew me as was her personal guard, nothing more.

"Alicia, Cooper. What should I do?" I squeezed my eyes shut and tried to focus on my job; not my sorrow. But that seemed impossible since all my job brought was grief.

It hurts. She still doesn't remember me. Her parents came
to visit today. She was not happy about that. It was hard
seeing them again and they clearly knew who I was and
remembered what I went through.

I was 12 so it's been 14 years. Nothing in Xan remembers
even in the slightest. She looks just like them. I wouldn't even need her name.

I've aged to 26 and I'm still tripping over my feet for a 14-year-old who never actually met me.

And it stings.

–GUARD JOURNAL OF

SERGEANT 7560

fifth 5742

The rest of the day came and went. I said goodnight to Jay and Xan. They wished me 'happy birthday' one last time and then I left and went to my room on the 5th floor. The layout of my room was like Xan's. It was just filled with more items.

I had my journal and pencil on my desk, along with two picture frames. One was of me and my parents and the other was of me and my older brother. On the floor beside my bed was my sketchbook and a small light yellow blanket with red seams.

I turned on the lamp above the wooden desk. It illuminated most of the room. Walking over to my bed, I picked up my pencil and sketchbook. The drawing I had been working on was a tall boy with a ponytail that reached his shoulders standing by a much younger boy with short spiky hair. It was almost finished. I just needed to add shading and some small details. I was copying an old picture that my mom had kept on her bedside table, but I didn't need the photo to know how to draw these people. Their image was burned into my mind.

I remember sitting down with my brother and him teaching me how to draw people and scenery. Each day I would learn something new. He was really good and I wanted to be just like him. So he started teaching me once I turned five.

I'd drawn various pictures over my lifetime and I'd filled many sketchbooks. I was getting better by the day.

My nerves were always pressured by tiny little voices that clouded my mind and drawing helped ease them. At least, a little.

"January 3rd," I whispered to myself. "That's the date. They've officially missed my 16th birthday." I rotated my pencil 180° and scratched away at an unwanted line. Then I brushed the eraser shavings off the paper with my hand. "Daniel would be...24...by now. Hmph. It really has been a long time." It took me a second before I could make my pencil move again. Most of the drawing had been done in feather strokes so now I went back over and bolded the lines.

"One day...I'll be doing this out of here. I'll leave one day and then I can draw big pictures and use real paints to color them." I sighed and then laughed mockingly at myself. "I'm talking to myself...again."

The lamp flickered which was unusual.

Then I felt something brush my cheek. Hot air spewed down the back of my neck.

"*Sýntoma tha vgo,*" something whispered.

"The heck?!" I exclaimed. I looked around, but found nothing. Nobody. I was the only one in the room.

Mist

A high-pitched, bloodcurdling scream echoed throughout the LEFP. I recognized it immediately.

"XAN!"

Samrish is officially 16 years old. He is still boisterous, but I know the secrets he thinks he can hide. I can't tell, but I believe Xan has some big secret, too. She won't talk about her hand. It gets annoying because of the eagerness that tugs at my curiosity.
Maybe I can get her to take off her glove for like a truth-or-dare sorta thing. But, that could backfire and they could ask me w

Sixth   1863

A high-pitched, bloodcurdling scream echoed throughout the LEFP. I recognized it immediately.

"XAN!"

My pencil had left a line in my journal from the vocal impact that hit my ears and jerked my body. The stool screeched as it slid across the floor. I shut off the lamp and burst through the door, startling my slacking guard. I ran past him, already on my way to her room.

"WHERE ARE YOU GOING?!" he yelled.

"It's none of your business!" I yelled back. It was dark out and barely any prisoners were outside of their cells. My footsteps echoed loudly and clanged as the metal flooring rocked ever so slightly.

What in the world could have happened?! It's midnight and Xandralin finds it fun to get murdered?! God, I hope she didn't get murdered. Please be fine, Xan. Maybe...maybe she had...I don't know, a really horrific nightmare?

But deep inside of me, I knew it was something deeper. Something even more terrifying than a stupid dream.

I reached the stairs that led up to Floor 3. My footsteps were masked by someone else's at the same speed. Rowan. No doubt about it. He must've heard her scream, too.

I didn't realize how close he was until I almost ran into him.

"*Ahk!*" he yelled, jerking backwards and barely avoiding me.

" 'Ahk' yourself, now come on." We ran together down to her room. Her door was open and Lijin wasn't standing at his post. I stopped. My feet planted themselves into the floor and my stomach dropped down into my toes in shock of what I saw inside her room

"...!!!" Rowan gasped. He sounded as horrified as I felt.

Lijin was a few feet away from her bed, arms outstretched and frozen. Next to him, slumped on the floor, there was a young girl. She was on her knees and her arms and hair draped down limply. There was blood on her hands and the floor. Everything was messed up. Loose papers were scattered throughout the room. Streaks of blood lined the walls. The girl's body started shaking violently. The black glove on her left hand signified that it actually was Xan who had screamed.

"What...what *happened?!*" I asked, terrified. Her head snapped up and I could see her face. Tear tracks ran down from her eyes and blood ran down from her mouth and nose. Her irises had lost color and wavered when she saw us. Rowan stepped towards her.

"NO!" Lijin yelled at him. "Don't get close to her!" Rowan froze and then took a few steps back until he was realigned with me.

"Why?!" I demanded. Xan stared at me. Her eyes welled again. *What happened to you?* She seemed to read what I was thinking.

"He knows!" Xan cried, shaking her head and sending tears flying. "Lijin knows! He knows what happened, but he won't tell me!" The desperate tone of her voice made me forget who I was looking at.

"Lijin–"

"Listen, it's best not to think of it. The paramedics are already on their way up here. They'll take care of her."

"But–" I tried to protest, annoyed that he had cut me off.

"Xan. Will. Be. Fine."

"...?" It startled me, the way he said it. There was longing in his voice like he was praying for it to be true.

He turned to face me. He was silent, but looked ready to propose something that could change our lives. Lijin's eyes told me one thing: *accept my next offer.* So I waited for him to speak.

"Rowan, Jaymon, stay after and help me fix up the room." He used my full name. He was dead serious about this.

"S-sure," I responded. It was an abrupt and suspicious question, but I accepted anyway. Beside me, Rowan didn't answer. He just stared at Xan's pitiful state. I nudged him with my shoulder, attempting to get him to say something.

"Oh, uh, yeah...sure...whatever."

"Stop..." Xan whimpered.

"Stop what–"

"STOP! I'm not a stupid child! You all have pity towards me and I don't want it!" She stood up, using the bed for support. She was filled with unusual outrage. She had never been like this before. And it caught me by surprise.

"Xan, we don't have...–we don't think you're weak or anything," I tried to explain, "we're just trying to help fix the situation."

"WELL I DON'T NEED HELP!!"

I heard footsteps run down the hall and stop right before the door. Rowan and I stepped to the side so we didn't block it.

Nobody came in. The door was wide open. They were just awaiting permission. "E-enter," Lijin called. A team of paramedics filed into the room. One of them–a woman in a white suit and mask–tried to grab Xan's arm. Xan yanked it away.

"Don't touch me!" she snarled. *What is going on with her? First... whatever happened here and now she's losing her character?*

She walked out with them, barely keeping her balance. As she started for the door, I noticed something about her left arm. There were burn marks all the way up her sleeve. Then, out of the blue, violet returned to her eyes. And then she collapsed. I was amazed at how prepared the paramedics were for this. One of them caught her, carefully arranging her left arm and hand away from their grip. Then they laid her limp body down on a stretcher that two of them brought in from the hallway.

How...did they...know...?

They walked out and shut the door.

"Lijin," Rowan immediately said, "*what is going on?*" Lijin sighed.

"You boys might wanna sit down for this."

● ● ●

The light was on and me and Rowan were on the floor while Lijin sat on the bed. His arms were crossed and his eyes were closed. Rowan's expression was pure jittery anticipation and my patience was running thin in the thick silence.

Finally, Lijin said something, "Have you boys ever heard of the Dragon Of The Mist?"

"The what-now?" Rowan asked at the same time that I responded with, "Never heard of it."

"The Dragon Of The Mist is one of the 5 Great Terrors; Wind, Flame, Earth, Mist, and Spirit. They were Greek demons that took over our world thousands of years ago.

"Each were sealed inside of the Vault of Eternal Darkness by a man name Kanobi. But, not long ago, Mist broke free. To seal it back inside the Vault, would release the rest of the Terrors. So...it was given to...a human... vessel. A seal was placed on the human so that it would not escape." His voice went quiet and he seemed to say the next part more to himself than to us. "After such a long time, it isn't that big of a surprise that it would try to break free."

"Wait–I don't understand," I said. "What does this have to do with Xan?"

"Jaymon," Lijin responded, getting more serious than I believed his nature allowed, "Xan *is* the vessel. She just doesn't know it."

"...!"

"...!!"

"What..." Rowan whispered, "what happened here?"

"The Dragon Of The Mist was trying to escape its vessel; thus making the seal spread throughout her body and placing Xan in more pain than she's ever endured."

I was in enough shock to have my heart pick up pace and my stomach churn. I swallowed the foul emotion and forced my stiff tongue to caress letters.

"The blood is from...her body tearing itself apart," I realized aloud. The guard nodded.

"She won't remember the event, but she will the pain. And it'll only get worse from here on out. I won't go into too much detail because the knowledge places both of you in danger, but her seal is passed from generation; she isn't Mist's first vessel so her seal isn't at full power. Once it realizes that, it'll do everything it can to get out. The pain will get worse and if we can't stop it..." He paused and swallowed audibly. "Xan will die and the world will go down with her."

"That's what her hand is," Rowan murmured. "It's the seal. People don't like her because they're scared of her. No. They're scared of what *inhabits* her."

"...How much time do we have?" I questioned, staring Lijin down.

"If I had to guess, we have until her 15th birthday–we have less than a month to try to replace her seal–"

"Or she dies," I choked. He nodded.

"...Or she dies. And the world goes up in flames."

My mind has been screwed with. Apparently my best friend has until February first to live unless we can give her a magical tattoo that'll trap the giant evil dragon or whatever that lives inside of her. Seven-year-old me would laugh at such nonsense-saying it's impossible but after what put me in the LEFP...I'm not so sure...

–PRISONER JOURNAL OF

SUBJECT 5742

Seventh   3029

The darkness retreated and I was in an obnoxiously white room with the strange echo of horrible pain. My arm felt like it was in pain, but felt fine at the same time. How was that possible? Maybe I was imagining things. I was planning on touching it just to make sure, until I was stopped in my tracks.

"...?" I tilted my head to the side and was shocked at my surroundings. I was in what looked like a hospital room, with machines and medical tools. My body was strapped to a metal table by bars. There was a crisp *whoosh* as a door slid open.

"...!"

"You're awake. *Great.*" The woman who stepped in rolled her eyes.

"Where am I?" I demanded.

"Calm your wits, you're still in your stupid prison." Her blonde ponytail bounced as she walked around the room writing God-knows-what down on her clipboard.

"It's not a room I've ever seen," I observed.

"That's because it's underground. This place has fourteen floors. Six for prisoners, six for guards, ground and sub. Never notice?"

"No," I said. "I've never gone below Ground Level."

"Ha. Well, you don't look like the type to venture." She shook her head in an exaggerated eye roll.

"I'm adventurous!" I drew in a breath at the weird anger that lit inside of me. I needed to focus. There were more important topics that I needed to attempt to cover. "Who are you and why am I here?"

"Who I am: classified. Why you are here: also classified," the woman chided. Great. So helpful. She grabbed a tablet off the counter and pressed a series of several buttons, then, swiping from bottom to top with two fingers, a hologram projected in front of her. *Whoa.*

"Stop putting your nose in my business, you snotty brat," she called, her back still to me. I let my body fall down onto the table so that I could only see the ceiling.

"I wanna know what happened. Why do I remember being in such horrible pain?" I asked after a brief period of silence. "I know that you have that knowledge." She sighed. *Very* dramatically.

"You mean you seriously don't know? Ha. Monsters really *don't* have brains." One of her words in particular sank in deep and crashed noisily when it hit my bones. '*Monsters*'. She had referred to me as a monster.

"I...I'm not a monster..." My voice betrayed me and cracked with emotion that usually neutralized once I realized it was there. But it didn't. For some anonymous reason, my emotions wouldn't subside. They just poured. *What is going on?!* "What do you know about me?!" I yelled.

"Not much, child. But I never asked you. And calm down. It wasn't an insult." She turned away and I swear I heard her mutter, "It's just the truth." Then the woman faced the open door and yelled a name that I had never heard before. It wasn't the name of a guard. I knew most guards by heart. This name was foreign. The person who walked in was a young boy, twenty at most, who gave off a very skittish impression.

"Yes, ma'am. I'm here, ma'am," he stuttered.

"Yeah, I noticed. Now get me the little freak's track record and data sheets."

"Want 'freak'?" I asked. "Hey, maid-boy, get her a mirror, too."

"Ah!!" It wasn't even that good of a comeback, but the woman took it like a bullet—which is what I wanted, by the way. "Stupid imbecile!!"

"I-I'll get the objects," the boy exclaimed, running out. Pathetic.

"Just the papers!!" she ordered.

"Don't forget the mirror!" I called, giggling at my own joke.

"THAT'S IT!" The woman slammed her hands down on the metal table that my body was strapped to. The action vibrated me. Her facial features were filled with rage. "I don't get paid enough to have to deal with freaks that belong in the circus. I'm one of the smartest people you will ever meet."

"Highly doubt it," I scoffed.

"Listen, psycho, I don't *like* kids. I am a mentally advanced scientific researcher who was forced to come to this pathetic prison wanna-be. You are a curse from the devil and I am an angel sent from God. You are *not* going to disrespect me unless you want it to be the last thing you'll do." I ignored her painful insults and honed in on the one truth in that entire speech.

I was a psycho.

"I'll say my goodbyes."

The boy re-entered the room and handed the woman her papers. "Here you go, ma'am." She took them and then cat-walked out of the room to read them away from me.

I yanked my arm up, shaking the table when the bar locked me down and startling the boy.

"Get. Me. Out," I hissed.

"I-I can't..." His eyes were fixated on my left hand. I hated it when people focused on my hand and not my face. Especially when I was trying to talk to them. It happened all the time. The only people I knew who could keep their interest hooked onto my words were Rowan, Jay, and Lijin.

"Hey! My eyes are up here!" I yelled. *What the heck is going on with me?! My emotions won't soothe. Why?*

"I-I'm s-sorry, miss, b-but I cannot l-let you out." I read the pathetic blubbering assistant's name tag. Hugo. There was no last name. I rolled with it anyway.

"Yes you can, Hugo with no last name provided. It's not that hard. Just unlock these." I looked down at my arms as I opened my fingers. Then something hit me when my eyes met his outfit. An idea bloomed. "You know what? C'mere." He was so hesitant it was funny. "Now," I demanded and he scurried over. I grabbed his shirt and pulled him down. "Listen here, bucko. I could kill you here and now if I felt like it. And each waking moment I spend staring at you has my curiosity growing. I wanna know how easy it'd be. I may be a kid, but you've forgotten that I was put in the Lunatic Encagement Facility Prison. Yeah, I'm crazy. Deal with it. And I have no problem turning this disgustingly white room red with your blood." I licked my lips. "Now get out if you aren't useful." I let go of his shirt and let him run out the door in a panic.

A moment later and I was sitting up with all limbs free, twirling his keys on my fingertips. "Too easy."

● ● ●

I snuck out of the room and went up a set of stairs that I assumed led to Ground Level. The stairwell let out in a dark room, but I could see perfectly fine. It was a closet with brooms and buckets and all the crap that janitors needed. Though, I thought of the room as unnecessary because most janitors wouldn't even dare to work here. It was too risky of a job in their eyes. I found the door and turned the knob, pulling towards me until it opened. Once it closed behind me, I ran. It was fuzzy, but I remembered seeing Jay, Rowan, and Lijin in between both of my blackouts. So they *had* to know what had happened. Right?

No one was outside of their cells because of the early hour. I had too much faith in that when I let my mind wonder.

Who was that woman? Why did she keep referring to me as 'monster' or 'freak'? How come I had to be strapped down? Why was there an echo of such terrible pain in my body?...Does it have something to do with my mark? What if-?

And I hit something and was jerked out of my scrambled thoughts. I was knocked backward and my feet misplaced the floor and I fell. I rolled down the stairs until my hand caught the railing and I was able to find my footing and jump onto it. The person attempting to get back on their feet at the top of the stairs was a small girl, clearly much younger than me.

She had short curly hair that was mostly dark brown, but had streaks of white in it. She had on the standard outfit of a prisoner and her neck read: 3014. Her features were petite so this was most likely her first year here. When she got to her feet and turned to face me, she gave off the impression of being scared of me. I mean, her green eyes seemed to ever so slightly shake with fear. And yet, she had a strong and harsh look to her. So maybe I had just startled her. I had certainly startled myself. My heart was beating faster than it was supposed to.

It took effort, but I was able to calm everything inside of me so that I could talk to the little girl.

"How come you're up so early? Shouldn't you be asleep?"

"My guard is annoying. I was looking for the knives," she responded in an almost robotic tone.

"...Uhm...okay...?" I didn't know how to respond to something like that.

"I am joking," she cleared. That relieved me a bit.

"Oh, ha-ha."

"So far."

"...Uhm...well, I, uh, this is my floor."

"Same. What is your name?"

"Xan."

"Greetings, Xan. I'm Lexi Widler." Her speech pattern was odd for someone her size, though I couldn't actually tell how old she was. I decided to ask about that one.

"Mind if I ask how old you are?"

"Yes, I do actually mind." There was a short period of awkward silence as she thought it over and I regretted asking. Then she shrugged. "But I shall tell you anyway. I am approximately nine years old," she told me.

"You don't sound like a 9-year-old," I noted, raising my eyebrow.

"Yes, well I am wise beyond my years," Lexi replied.

"I see." I smiled and hopped down from the metal railing to resume walking towards my room. Lexi took a step to her right and blocked my way.

"How long have you been here?" she questioned. It took me a second to decide on answering honestly.

"Over six and a half years. Why?" She looked taken aback by the amount of time I had spent at the LEFP. I mean, I didn't blame her. I still couldn't wrap my mind around the fact that I was supposed to be here for the rest of my life. It was a pretty long time to be alone...

"I have been here for a week. I intend on breaking out of here soon. Clearly you've never thought of that since you have lived here for more than 2372.5 days." I checked her math first and tilted my head in surprise at her quick calculations. Then I comprehended her words and shook my head in slight disapproval.

"I have thought of it. Many times. But I'd have nowhere to go." I shrugged off the thought. "I'm, uh, gonna go to bed. Night, Lexi." I marched past her.

"Goodnight..., Xan." I could feel her eyes track my movements as I scurried to my room. I assumed that I was out of what she thought was earshot when she whispered, "Alluring. This place beholds more characters than I thought it did." I rolled my eyes and coughed a laugh to myself. Then something hit me. 'Alluring' was a synonym for 'interesting'. Interesting. Not freaky. Or monstrous. She...she didn't think...I was weird or anything. Aside from three boys, this strangely smart girl was one of the only people who didn't get a freakish first impression of me. Maybe it was because it was dark out, but she was different. I could sense it. Honestly, I sensed the same thing in Rowan, Jay, and a bit of Lijin.

What if they were just so desperate to have someone to talk to that they forced themselves to overlook my flaws? That wasn't something that I was quite ready to consider. So, for now, they were just the only people who actually accepted who I was. Or what I was.

I turned back around to say something to Lexi, but she was already gone.

● ● ●

Lijin was slumped down on the floor with his back propped up against the wall when I reached him. One arm rested on his knee while the other on the ground. His baseball cap covered his face and it took me a second to realize he was asleep. Guards were given their own rooms. Once their subject fell asleep or a different guard took care of them for the night, they were allowed to return to their rooms to sleep in peace. I had been handed over to the crazy woman from Sub Level or wherever I was, so he could have gone back to his room. So why was he still here? Like he had been waiting on me or something?

I crouched beside him and looked up into his closed eyes. Behind his eyelids were bright blue black holes that sucked in imagery and sent it to the brain. Lijin's eyes sucked things in at a different angle than most people. 'Things' being, more precisely, me. He saw me in a kind and normal way. How come that was different from what everybody else saw? *What do you see in me that other people don't?* I wondered, scrunching my eyebrows together as I tried to make sense of it all. *Why don't you hate me like everyone else does? Why aren't you afraid of me?* I had wanted to ask these questions for a very long time, but I had buried them so deep that they never came to my mind again. And for a reason that I couldn't explain, all of the thoughts and feelings that I had desperately stored away over the past seven years were all starting to resurface.

My hand reached out to his shoulder on the sudden impulse to awake him from his sleep and ask him all of these questions. Then my hand caught my eye. It was the hand with the black fingerless glove. The hand with the strange marking on it. This hand was the reason that my parents had given me up and I was forced to live out my life in solitude. I was different. I was an outcast. And my stupid left hand was responsible for it all. I retracted my hand to my chest and let my heart waver in the pain that bringing all of this up caused. Then I opened my eyes, smiled, stood up, and entered my room.

Masking my true emotions was what I did best.

It was what I knew myself by.

Well apparently, I didn't know myself anymore because, for something not even I could *guess* at, as I shut my door and laid down on my bed, jealousy towards kids who weren't me welled up in pools of tears that spilled and hit the sheets.

"...*ung...kh...*" Weird sounding sobs tore at my throat until I gave in to this new baby inside of me and curled up into a ball and sobbed my heart out in rivers onto the sheets until darkness found me.

Day 9 of living here. I have spent time collecting data and I have discovered that my journal is read once I leave the room. I shall leave it alone, though and give you what you want. Today I met the most peculiar girl. She had fast but strange reflexes. I will not name her because you creeps should leave her alone. It was very dark out. One look at the way her eyes reacted and I could tell that she is advanced in the sense of sight. Unlike me who could barely make her out. This girl was clearly much older than me, but she did not talk to me as if I was born 4 years ago as some people do. She is different. I'm just not sure in what way.

–PRISONER JOURNAL OF

SUBJECT 3014

Eighth   5742

Honestly, I don't remember waking up and leaving my cell-ish. I, uh, just started remembering things once I was already seated at the table with Jay. We were waiting on Xan. I think that I could speak for both of us when I say that we were kinda scared to see her. I mean, the things we had learned about her... woof. I still couldn't comprehend most of it. And she herself didn't even know any of it.

"Are you okay?" Jay asked. My eyes focused on what was in front of me. Jaymon had his book out and open, but he was looking at me instead of it. I had his full attention. I snorted.

"Why wouldn't I be?"

"Xan's going to die in twenty-eight days?" I kicked him, feeling both his skin bruise and my toes crack.

"GOD." I pulled my foot up onto the seat of my chair and rubbed my toes. "Don't say that, Jay. Please...?"

"Yeah...and OW!" he complained.

"Sorry. I just...don't know what to do." I looked down.

"I get it. It's a big shock. We need more information. As much as I hate to admit it, Lijin has more info on this than anyone else will. He's our best bet at saving her."

"Yeah," I agreed.

"You know what I've noticed?" he asked in a quiet voice.

"What have you noticed?"

"Lijin knew everything about the Dragon, right? And how much do you want to bet that no one has ever heard of it besides knowing that it's in Xan? C'mon, man. Lijin has to have *some* type of connection to it. Right?" I analyzed his claim. Then I revised it.

"I mean, it's a possibility, sure. But we don't have enough evidence to pull a claim like that." I emphasized my words by twirling my hands around in the air. I could see it on his face that a part of him agreed with me.

Jay looked down, deep in thought. "It's hard to explain, but the way he said all those things tells me that he just skimmed the top of all the information he knows for the sake of telling it as a story."

I considered it, but my thoughts were interrupted by the sound of a chair sliding across the tile. I looked up to the side, expecting to see Xan and a bit surprised that she hadn't said anything. I was shocked to find that sitting beside me wasn't a girl, but a male guard.

"I hate to intrude on your conversation, but I need to talk to you guys." The young and familiar voice was clouded by the prep of harsh words. Lijin folded his hands atop the table.

"First things first...she isn't coming."

"Why not?" Jay demanded. Lijin sighed and held up his hand.

"I'm getting there. I was asleep outside her door and I woke up to a noise that didn't particularly belong. I, uh, was trying to figure out what it was when I noticed that it was coming from her room. She was sobbing. I went to knock on the door when I heard a strange voice. '*Sýntoma tha vgo,*' it said."

"What does that mean?" I asked.

" 'I will be out soon.' I didn't go into the room. Can you guess why?"

"It's Greek. Isn't it?" I stared into his eyes as sweat ran down the back of my neck. "*The Dragon Of The Mist is one of the 5 Great Terrors; Wind, Flame, Earth, Mist, and Spirit. They were Greek demons that took over our world thousands of years ago.*" The thing inside of Xan was Greek. Then my mind went back even farther. Wait...I had heard the exact same words right before she screamed.

"I heard it say that last night," I announced.

"Come to think of it...I also remember hearing such a thing," Jay added.

"It's not a good sign," Lijin told us. "It worries me." His face flinched with unspoken pain. "W-we may not have all the time that we thought we did."

"What?! We barely had any time!! W-what are we going to do?!" I cried. Lijin waved his hand at me.

"Calm down, Rowan. It's hard to believe, but I have some kind of idea on what I'm doing. But, this leads us to the next problem—"

Jay cut him off. "Yeah, about that, I've been wondering…" he pulled his legs up onto his seat to rest his arm on his knee, "what *is* your connection to all of this?" Lijin's eyebrows raised slightly, almost in surprise. "I mean, you know so much and everyone else knows so little. What's up with that?"

The guard looked down and his aura shifted to scary. "I have no connection. I just used to hear a lot of stories from my mom. Moving on, Xan is falling apart. The events of the past twenty-four hours—not even—are causing small emotions to rise. Any negative emotion strengthens the grip that Mist has on her. The emotions become more severe and the more severe she lets them grow, the stronger her demon gets. This leads to Xan remembering things she doesn't want to, which causes stronger emotion. Then the clock ticks faster. We are running out of time."

Somewhere in the middle of all that, I transferred to panic-mode.

"W-we didn't have any time to begin with!!"

"Rowan! Stop spiraling! There's a cure." I forced myself to hush.

"There's a cure?" Jay repeated as he leaned in.

"Yes. We'll have to perform a ritual."

"A ritual?" Jay questioned in utter shock.

"Yes. Just...one problem..." He faded off.

"Well?" I pushed. "What's the problem?" He looked up at me.

"I can't remember what we need or how to perform it.," Lijin admitted. Jay and I groaned in sync.

"Where'd you first learn?" Jay asked.

"My mom. She told me almost everything I know about the 5 Great Terrors."

"Okay, then we just ask her."

"Problem...I-I can't..." His voice faltered and he didn't continue. I understood immediately. She was gone. There was no one to ask. Jay seemed to pick up on the same conclusion.

"No biggie. W-we can just do research. There's bound to be something since they're so famous," I suggested.

"On what device, Rowan?" Jay questioned. "On what device?"

"...Uhm..." I hadn't thought that far yet. "We could ask somebody who knows?" Jay rolled his eyes. We had literally just gone over how nobody knew any details about Mist. I was just running my mouth about false hopes by now. But I couldn't bring myself to actually believe that.

"You're hopeless, you know that?"

"Actually...there is someone else who would know," Lijin announced in a low voice. When I looked at him, he was staring into his lap and fidgeting with his gloves. He looked so young. Honestly, it almost scared me.

"Who?"

"M–er–Xan's mom."

"Then we can ask her," Jay said. Lijin snorted.

"Doubtful. You see, she doesn't really like me. I have...history...with the Raq family. Xan's parents don't take kindly to me and I don't take kindly to them. I, uh, actually flipped them off yesterday. Ha-ha. So, yeah. I mean, we can try, but there's no promised success." I was a little shook that he had flipped them off, but I got over it quickly.

"We can't give up..." My voice shook. I gazed downward to find my hands trembling.

Lijin's head snapped up to look at me. "We won't," he responded automatically. "We'll figure it out." Jay and I nodded. "Aren't you boys gonna eat?" Lijin questioned.

"Not hungry," Jay replied.

"Ah." He stood up. "You guys should go see her. I don't know what happened, but something hit her pretty hard. Just one thing." I saw Jaymon tear his eyes up to focus on what the guard was saying. "Are you listening?"

"Yes," we both responded.

"Do not bring up her demon. At all. It will give way to feelings you can't even dream of. That will weaken her to the point of breaking. Letting that loose is like opening the gates to hell. It's suicide. Whether you believe me or not." And he walked away.

● ● ●

I hesitantly pressed my knuckles to the wood. Then I drew my hand back and tapped the wood again. Then again. And then again. Then again-

Jay smacked my hand. "Stop knocking!"

"What if she can't hear me?" I asked.

"She can! Trust me. Just give her a second." Sure enough, there were footsteps followed by an angry sweep of the door. Xan's eyes were puffy and red; a frame that didn't fit her picture.

"Lijin, I said–!!" Once she realized that she wasn't yelling at the culprit of the crime, Xan reached out, grabbed the door handle, and slowly pulled it back towards the inside of the room until it clicked shut. Jay and I exchanged confused glances.

"..."

"...?"

When the door opened again, Xan was her old self. Calm and laid-back. Happy. -Ish.

"Hi," she said. Her cheeks burned a vibrant red. "Sorry."

"A-are you...alright?" I asked.

"Y-yeah."

Me and Jay entered the room, glancing at each other, and Xan closed the door behind us. The room looked pretty normal. There was no lingering trace of what had happened. After Lijin had explained everything and answered most of our questions, we had spent around an hour straightening this place up. I was drained by the end.

"Xandralin," Jaymon said sitting on her bed. She spun away from her desk to face him, clearly startled by the name he had used.

"Yeah?" she answered.

"What happened?" She looked down and touched the desk with the fingers of her left hand. Then her hand clenched up, her knuckles turning white. I still wanted to know the origin behind that hand. There were visible lines on her fingers, but I had a feeling there was more. Sure, I knew that it was what kept the Dragon Of The Mist at bay, but what did it really look like? And though I wouldn't admit it aloud, I had the same hunch as Jay. We didn't have the full story.

When the girl in front of me looked back up, she was smiling and there was no evidence of the indecision that I had just witnessed. "Nothing happened. I was actually going to ask both of you the same thing about last night. I know you were there. I remember that much." Jay eyed me.

"Well…" I started. Though, me starting and fading off just made the situation more suspicious. *Dang it, Rowan.*

"I wanna know." she repeated.

"I'm trying to recall it all," I lied. Last night had permanently engraved itself into a little spot in my brain. It was hard to look at her and the room without it replaying itself. But I couldn't say anything. Lijin had said to not bring it up.

"It was seven hours ago," Xan pointed out.

"I-I was tired. I didn't comprehend it all easily." Now that was only partially a lie.

"What is 'it'? What couldn't you comprehend?" I looked to the other guy in the room, desperate for backup. He closed his eyes and nodded slightly. "I got it," he mouthed.

"You screamed so we came to see if you were okay. You were having a nightmare and you jerked your body in a way that it isn't supposed to move so the paramedics had to take you." Simple, but I guess it worked.

"But–"

"That's what I remember. Not really sure it's able to not align."

"I-I second that," I exclaimed.

"…" Xan fell silent. Sweat ran down my back. "You know, it's kinda funny…" she whispered.

"What is?" Jay asked.

"When I asked what happened...both of your heart rates sped up by a lot. Rowan breathed in an unusual pattern. And Jay's pulse rocketed. I don't know what your motives are, but..." She turned to face us, her eyes shadowed. "...I can't believe that you guys would lie to me."

"...!" I was completely surprised. Since when could she track heart beats?!

"Xan–" Jay tried to explain, but she just stepped to the door. She opened it and motioned to the rest of the prison.

"I would like to be left alone. I'll talk to you guys later."

"Wait, we–"

"LEAVE!" she screamed, a show of what Lijin had described about her emotions growing with every tick of our cruelly fast clock. She covered her mouth. When her hands fell she muttered, "Just leave...please." I sighed in guilt and left the room. Jay followed. Xan shut the door without even glancing at us. Though I couldn't hear someone's pulse, I could hear her body slide down the door and shake with sobs.

This wasn't the Xan I knew. Where had *she* gone?

different
it's what everything now is
the clock ticks too fast
the days used to seem bright
but as of now, good times have sank into the past
my brain's memory masker
has lost all its cast
it's barely been a day
but i can't remember when i was happy last

the gun was in my hand
and i unknowingly aimed it at my head
i don't feel comfortable anymore
can't trust what is said

heh-heh
i'm turning into a psycho
i aim between the eyes and count down
1, 2, 3,...and i shoot on 'go'

–PRISONER JOURNAL OF

SUBJECT 3029

ninth 7560

"TERAKI!!"

"Yes?" I asked, looking up.

"You have a call."

"Couldn't they have just called my cell?"

"Are you going to take it or what?!" Innkuro demanded. She waved to the stairs. "I have them on hold." I sighed and stood up, leaving the comfort of my room. I walked with Innkuro down to a small office. Inside was a desk with monitors and stacks of paper. And also an old-school white telephone with a blinking red light on it. I still didn't understand why we had these and not normal up-to-date phones.

I was wondering who the heck would call me on one of our work phones and not my personal cell-phone when Innkuro shut the door. I sat down in the leather chair and picked up the phone.

"Hello?" I asked.

"*Li Li!*" a little girl's voice screamed. "*Li Li, you answered!*"

"Litz?" I was genuinely shocked.

"*Yeah! Are you surprised? I got the number from Mommy's phone!*"

"Litz," I rubbed my face and looked up at the ceiling, "does Mommy *know* that you have her phone?"

The little girl paused. "*No.*"

I heard a distant voice join the call. "*Who are you talking to, Litz?*"

"*Li Li!*" I groaned, but neither heard me.

"*Oh, cool. Sup, Lijin.*"

"Hi, Sam." Litz was five years old and clung to me like a pet monkey. If monkeys could squeal your name at the top of their lungs, that is. And Sam was twelve, a weird and awkward preteen who I still couldn't figure out.

"Guys, can I talk to you later? I have a lot to deal with right now."

"*Oh, come on,*" the older girl moaned. "*You say that every time. We miss you.*" I smiled, thinking about the last time I had seen them. That was probably way back on Memorial Day of last year. I hadn't been able to make Thanksgiving, Christmas, or New Years, so it had been a while. I truly did miss them.

"I miss you, too, but I-I have work to do. Put your mom on for a moment first, though, okay?"

"*Fiiiine.*" Sam yelled for her mother and then the phone was transferred.

"*Hello?*"

"Hey, Mei. It's Lijin. I just wanted to let you know that your daughters had called me in the middle of work on *your phone.* Try to keep it in your reach."

"Sorry... You sound so drained. Are you alright?" Should've known. I had lived with Mei for around thirteen years. She gave off major mom-vibes. She fostered a lot of kids. Four so far. And she adopted three. Sam and Litz were adopted when they were really little so they probably didn't remember their real parents. Unlike unlucky me.

"I-it's my subject. We're having a...*problem* with her."

"...Tell me who she is again?"

"Xandralin Raq," I told her.

"...'Raq' you say? Is it..." She faded off.

"I've talked about her before. I mean, this is my 4th year here. And yes. It, uh, it actually is." I traced random patterns on the smooth desk. It took her a second to respond. The silence screwed with my nerves.

"Wow." Mei fell silent again.

I lowered my voice. "Her seal is weakening. We've already had an attempted escape just last night. Her emotions are out of control and her physical strength will soon start to increase. I can't remember how to do the ritual to replace her mark. And..." I banged my head on the table. "And I used to know every detail, but now it's all fuzzy."

"*Let me think. Well, you know where Abagail lives, correct?*" Mei questioned. I lifted my head.

"Yeah. Just a neighborhood over from you. If that," I responded.

"*So, close, huh? And she knows how to do it?*"

"Yes. Well, in theory anyway. But, I can't just march over and ask her. She doesn't like me. And I'm not even sure if I can get away with the ritual here at the LEFP."

"*You could do it here.*"

"I mean, yeah, sure." Then my brain actually processed her request. "Wait, what? I can't do that! I'd have to sneak her out! And her little friends; they wouldn't leave her for crap."

"*How many kids? In total, including her?*"

"Th-three."

"*Okay. Now hear me out, son.*" I put the phone on speaker so that I could stand and pace the room. "*You bring all three here. I ask Abagail since she shouldn't really have anything against me. We can do the ritual in the abandoned tunnel way so that she has lots of space. You guys can stay for a bit and then you sneak them back into the LEFP if possible. Or we could figure something else out later. Yes, there's flaws, but it would work, right?*"

I thought it over. "Maybe. But I don't know how to get them out without the Head Guard noticing."

"You're more advanced in smarts and problem-solving than most people I know. You can figure it out along the way."

"But I don't know if I can actually pull it off," I protested.

"Lijin, I know how much she means to you. We'll figure something out–" The door opened.

"Lijin? A, uh, guard named Innkuro told us you'd be in here. She also said to make sure you know that she helped give us directions to you, since apparently that's so freaking important." I turned to them.

"Rowan? Jay?"

"Are those her friends?" Mei asked.

"Yeah, uhm, Mei, I have to go," I told her. I walked back over to the phone. I put my hand up to it, ready to end the call.

"Alright. Good luck. Love you. You don't have to respond." Then she hung up before I could.

"Ooh-ooh. Was that your girlfriend?" Rowan joked lightly.

"Not even close," I scoffed.

"Then who was she?" Jay questioned, hands in pockets. I didn't feel like explaining it. Though I had nothing against her, I didn't think of Mei as what her legal title implied.

"Someone. Now, what did you guys come for?"

"Well," Rowan started, "we went to see Xan like you suggested. She was...different. She looked horrible then shut the door and looked fine in moments. Then she started acting a bit weird like staring at her hand and desk. Then she asked about last night."

You didn't tell her, did you?! I was about to yell when I was cut off. "So we came up with a story that covered the gist of it," Jay continued. "But she saw right through us."

"...?" Saw right through them?

"She was tracking our heart rates as we spoke so that she knew when the lies started. I knew that her hearing was good, but not *that good*. She penetrated flesh and muscle and was able to single out the pattern of our hearts. All the while, all three of us were talking so there was additional noise. Isn't that just a *little* abnormal to you?"

"As the veil between human and monster thins, they conjoin," I murmured as I sat down.

"What?"

"As the veil between human and monster thins, they conjoin," I repeated. It was something I'd heard on various occasions. I hated all of those occasions. Those words always came from people I didn't like. Though I liked few people so it could come from anyone at this point.

"You mean...it's merging with her or something?" Rowan's voice shook. Poor kid. He was terrified. They probably both were. But Jay was better at hiding it.

"She'll just advance in senses and skills," I explained. "Soon enough it'll fully take over and then break out, killing her in the process." The last part left something bitter in my mouth. I swallowed it down.

"How far are you on the ritual?" Jay pushed.

"I might have a place for it, but not much else."

"Where's the place?"

"...That lady's house."

"But that's outside of the LEFP," he pointed out.

"No! Really?! I thought it was next to our secret treehouse in the basement!" I sassed.

"You guys have a secret treehouse?" Rowan asked, clearly confused.

"Sarcasm, idiot," Jay told him. "They don't have a basement either."

"Oh."

"Guys, I know it'll be hard, but I need you two to try and keep her calm. We lose time with the greater her emotions get," I reminded them. Why was it that that always succeeded at closing my throat?

"Yeah, but like...*how?*" He slid down the side of a shelf to sit on the floor with his legs crossed and bangs swaying. Jay stared at Rowan, doing what I figured was contemplating whether or not he should join him until he turned to me to hear my answer.

"I dunno," I said honestly. I thought about it for a second. "You guys could–"

"Teraki, you don't live in there!!" Innkuro called. "Get out if you're done!" Her tall figure appeared as a shadow then opened the door. She pointed behind her, signifying for us to leave. Rowan and I stood up and the three of us exited the small office.

"Man, you're looking like you need a drink after talking to them," Innkuro commented. She did a terrible job at getting me to like her in the same way she *clearly* likes me. And she was annoying. Also, we aren't allowed to leave or have drinks in case of getting wasted. So did she really have a way to get us what I assumed was alcohol? I really didn't want to find out.

"Well, I'm feeling like I need therapy after listening to you," I groaned. She didn't take it in the way I wanted her to. She lost no confidence. Sadly.

"I can take you out for a drink. What do you say?" What was it with her? Like, I seriously wondered if she was mentally sane.

"No."

"Oh, come on. You sure?"

"Yes."

"Seriously? You're no fun."

"Get back to work, Innkuro." She huffed and walked away. Good riddance. She was too persevering. She needed to learn to take a hint. Actually, it wasn't even a hint. I had flat out told her on countless occasions. And yet, here we are.

"Like I was saying," I told the boys when we resumed walking and I was sure no one could hear me, "you guys could get her into something simple. L-like music."

"Where are we supposed to get things like that?" Jay asked, his visible eyebrow raised.

"My room," I responded without hesitation.

"Ha. *You* listen to music?" I almost laughed. Music used to be the biggest thing in my life. Now I almost couldn't stand it.

"Yeah."

"They don't allow subjects in sergeants' rooms," Rowan reminded. His gaze was focused on his pale feet.

"I can give it to you. Then we leave."

"What's 'it'?" I didn't respond. I just continued walking. There was a few minutes of silence before a prisoner passed by us and muttered, "Ooh, the trouble starters finally get punished." Jay punched him within milliseconds.

"Jaymon!" I yelled, keeping up protocol for such actions.

"What?" The unawareness in his voice was much like a child's.

"Y–!..." I faded off. Who was I kidding? It wasn't like I had the guts to actually punish the kid. He meant too much to her. "Never mind," I sighed.

The stairs rattled as our feet hit them. Rowan's eyes danced around, careful to not make eye contact with anyone that passed by. Jay stayed silent. Before I knew it, I had led the boys to my room.

"Here," I said. And I opened the door. The interior was filled with papers and special items that guards were required to have including communication devices, a baton, a small .22 caliber pistol, an ID card, etc. There was the small indistinguishable click of metal being removed from its resting place.

"Rowan!" I scolded, spinning around and catching him with the gun in his hand. He slowly set it down, shocked that I knew it was him without turning around first.

"Why do you own a gun?" he asked. I shrugged.

"Supposed to own one." I went over to my bed and picked up a small silver box. It fit into the palm of my hand and was thin enough to fit in any pocket without any trace that it's there. I took it back over to the boys.

"Look," I tapped a button to power it on and then slid two fingers across the small screen until a hologram lit up in the air, "all she has to do is scroll through and find a song. Once she does," I opened a latch on the side and pulled out two circular speakers that were about the size of my fingertips, "she puts these in her ears and hits 'PLAY'. They're so tiny, no guard will notice, but she won't lose them because there are built-in trackers that link to the main box." I snapped the speakers back in and watched the blue hologram disappear when I turned it off. I handed it over to Rowan and he shoved it into his pocket.

"Th-thanks. Now about the ritual–"

"I've got it. You guys keep her calm and restrained and I'll figure out the rest," I reassured.

"Got it," Jay said. "But, uh, do you really think she'll let us talk to her right now? I mean, she seemed pretty mad when we lied to her."

"Xan has no one other than you guys and I know you know that. She'll come around. Just give her time." They both nodded. I smiled then opened the door.

"You guys should go before your guards come looking for you."

"Right."

"Are you going back to your post at Xan's door?" Rowan asked.

"Yes," I told him. "I'm just going to stay here and think for a few minutes. See if I can, uhm, figure something out for the ritual. Then I'll go back to her room."

"Okay." He looked down.

"Rowan?" Jay asked softly.

"I, uh, just really want Xan to be okay. She's different. I don't even recognize her anymore. Lijin, she cries. She's been tough and scary for a long time, but now......You better be able to fix her. And she better not die." He left the room. Jay followed.

"I want to. More than you know," I whispered. Something fell down my cheek. "Dang it, Mist. You've taken everything." I shut the door, turned from it, then hit the wall. "No," I told myself. "Not Xan. She's all I have left and I refuse to lose her."

I walked over to my desk to put my hands on it and leaned my head over to pinch my eyes shut.

I will save her. No matter the consequence.

first day in this crap hole and I'm already sick of it. okay, I'm sick of the people. okay, I'm sick of one person. adrian something-something. he beats up kids for weird reasons and I think he wants me to, too. Maybe. people get on my nerves so I guess I'll do what I want. I'm all about making a name for myself and 'psycho badass' is just my style. this kid keeps talking about a freakish girl. she makes perfect bait.

Arabi T.

tenth 3029

They came back and knocked on my door. I didn't answer and I kinda expected them to open it anyway. But they didn't. They respected my boundaries and stayed outside my room.

"Xan," Rowan said, "we, uh, aren't gonna force you to let us in. 'Cause we shouldn't have lied to you. But, we have something for you. Here." A little silver box slid into my room from under the wooden door. I got up from my spot on my bed and, after just a second or two of walking, held it in my hands. It had a small screen and hinges on one of the sides.

"What is it?" I voiced accidentally.

"Just fiddle with it," Jay replied. "You'll figure it out." That helped.

I rolled my eyes. "Thanks." I smiled, watching their shadows. Then I leaned my forehead against the door. "I know that last night has something to do with my mark. And that it's probably really important. But, if it required you guys to shield a truth that could help me possibly understand literally everything about my life, then I won't push it," I said sarcastically.

"Well, when you put it like that..." Rowan replied. We laughed. Then the weird hatred that had consumed me disappeared as abruptly as it had shown up. There was definitely something going on with me. Something was wrong with me. My emotions were out of control. It was new. And I didn't like it.

"I-I'm sorry," I apologized.

"We're sorry, too," they said together. I stood up and opened the door. I held up the box and looked at it.

"Well, uh, thanks for...whatever this is. Now, seriously. What the heck is it?" They gave off whole-hearted smiles and nervous laughs.

"Not sure what the official title is, but it's like a pocket radio," Jay explained, rubbing the back of his neck.

"It'll be lunch in around an hour. We'll leave you till then." Rowan waved and started for his room with Jay traveling close behind with his hands in his pants' pockets.

"Seeya." I took the box to my desk. The latch looked like it opened so I dug my nails under it and pulled up. Inside were two small speakers. After a moment's hesitation, I placed one of them in my right ear. Then I hit the 'POWER' button on the side. The screen lit up with small words that said 'SWIPE UP'. So, I took two fingers to the device and slid upward like the woman from that morning had. A hologram projected into the air. It was wavy at first, but then it solidified. I scrolled through the pop ups of unusual names until I gave up on figuring out what they were and clicked one. Someone else's voice filled my ear with instrumental music playing in the background.

They were song titles.

I paused the one that was playing and scrolled through until I found something promising. I let it play and shoved the portable radio in my pocket. I left my desk to sit down on my bed and let the sound of the vocalist carry me from the crazy events that I had undergone in the past few hours. I let my body slip down to lay on the mattress. I pressed my hand to my chest and closed my eyes.

The words left my lips in a whisper, "Thanks, guys."

● ● ●

The bell rang, which caused me to cover my ears. When the noise concluded and I was able to drop my hands, I took out the music thingy from my pocket and stopped the song that was playing in the middle of its chorus. I would have laid there for hours, just listening, but I couldn't today. The bell meant that it was lunch time. Time to finally get up and talk to Rowan and Jay. With that, I got out of bed and went to my bathroom. I entered the room to look at my reflection. I was surprised to find that the ear bud was invisible to the naked eye. That would become useful. But, for now, I'd leave all of it in my room.

I took out the ear bud, placed it in its case, then opened the bottom drawer under the sink. When it slid open, an orange, label-less bottle rolled forward. The small amount of things inside of it rattled. I scowled. I'd forgotten that was in here. It was almost empty, but there was still about twenty pills inside. I slammed the drawer shut and then set the music box in one of the other wooden drawers. I left the bathroom, closing its door behind me. I could sense Lijin outside.

I opened the door with caution, getting a feeling that I shouldn't test him this time. Lijin was standing against the wall, his arms tightly crossed. He must have been deep in thought, I suppose, but he wasn't much of the serious type. Honestly, it kind of scared me.

"Lijin?" I whispered. With a start, he snapped out of whatever thoughts he was in and turned to face me.

"Oh, hey, Xan. You finally get hungry?" he asked with a kind smile that hid everything that I'd just seen.

"Yeah, I guess. I'm meeting Rowan and Jay in the cafeteria, so I've gotta get going. Goodbye..." He waved, but then immediately returned to his state of thought, spacing off once again. Something bad was going on. Rowan and Jay couldn't talk to me without their hearts racing and Lijin was getting more serious by the minute. What had happened last night?

I decided to forget for now. *Later,* I told myself. *I'll worry later. There's no need to work myself up over it right now.* But I still couldn't help the way that my stomach kept slowly fluttering around and tying into knots at the thought of it.

I was bounding down the stairs when I noticed a young girl with short bouncy brown and white curls a bit in front of the bottom of the stairwell. That at least brought some type of smile to my face. I felt some kind of emotion other than numb confusion.

I caught up to her quickly. "Hey, Lexi!" I smiled larger, trying everything in my power to look jovial for the little girl.

"Oh. Greetings, Xan. I was moving to the cafeteria. Would you like to accompany me?" Her bright green eyes reflected thousands of little lights from every light around us, created by electricity and the sun.

"Sure," I agreed, enjoying the company.

The young girl stared at me as we walked. She tried to be discreet, but I noticed her. We made small talk as much as possible, but it usually ended in my silence and her glances. I despised the extra attention, but didn't necessarily feel like saying anything. Her emerald eyes drifted to my hand, just like everyone else's. My heart speeding up in fear of judgment, I pushed it behind my back, out of her line of sight.

"I'd like to introduce you to my friends," I announced, desperate for something to talk about that didn't involve my hand or glove. Or me in general, if it came down to it. But I could deal with the boys. That topic was fine with me.

"Delightful," she replied, grinning. "How many of them are there?"

"Two. They're a little bit older. They don't tend to like many people and get into quite a lot of trouble. But, I think they might like you. Just give them time. Though, don't call the emo-looking one 'emo'. He doesn't like that and you might be murdered on the spot." I shrugged.

"...?" She seemed to be wondering if she should be concerned or not. It was a joke, but Lexi looked to be taking it seriously.

When we entered the lunch room, Rowan and Jay were at our usual table, just a little bit off to our right. Rowan noticed me first so I waved as we headed towards them. Lexi hung back a bit, either scared of them because of what I'd just said or because she'd never met them before. Jay eyed her suspiciously. Rowan just stared at Jay.

"Guys, this is Lexi," I introduced. "She's new. I met her last night." Jay raised his eyebrows.

"Last night?" he questioned.

"Last night, this morning, same thing. It was dark out." I waved off his question and turned to Rowan who was watching this all go down in curiosity. "Anyway, Lexi, this is–"

"Rowan Samrish." He held out his hand. She reluctantly took it. And then, because she couldn't possibly feel more intimidated or put on the spot, Rowan proceeded to ask, "So? What'd you do to get in, kid?" She took a step back, unsure of how to answer such an upfront question.

"Rowan!" I complained. He just glanced at me quickly, grinning.

"I-I," Lexi stammered, regaining her voice, "I pushed a classmate into the habitat of starving lions at the zoo on a field trip. They were annoying me and it made me feel complete to get to observe them getting mauled to death. Though, I am surprised that they sent me here of all places." She looked around.

"Cool," Rowan said, nodding in respect. When Lexi had completed her examination of the room, her eyes landed on Jay. He hadn't introduced himself. She waited patiently for a name.

"Jaymon Rivereay." She put out her hand, thinking that he would do the same as Rowan in their greeting. He just snarled, "Touch my hand and you *will* lose your fingers." She laughed nervously and withdrew her hand.

"Okay then," she whispered to herself. I leaned forward and lowered my voice so that they would be the only ones who could hear me.

"Hey, can she sit with us? Please? She's young, new, and I don't think she has anyone else to sit with or talk to." I gave her a quick glance that she didn't notice.

"How come? Why do you seem to like her so much?" Jay asked in return. I shrugged, half-expecting the question.

"I don't know. She doesn't ignore me or make fun of me. She-she isn't scared. When I met her she was kind and talked to me as if it wasn't one in the morning and I was walking around the prison by myself. It's rare that I find people like that and I want to keep her for as long as I can," I explained.

"I'm cool with it," Rowan said. Jay rolled his eyes.

"Fine. We can see how it goes," he caved. I smiled. I liked how easily he'd give in if he knew that it made me happy. It was a hidden character trait that he had. He valued his friends' feelings. I turned to the girl.

"Lexi, do you want to, uh, maybe take a seat? Eat with us?" I offered.

"How could I resist such a thing?" And she sat down in the only empty seat. It was across from Jay and beside me and Rowan. Since Jay seemed deadly in her eyes, it was the only chair at the round table that provided the most protection.

"Nice. I'm glad that you feel comfortable sitting with us. It's not often that we have others at the table," I laughed. Then my ears caught something. Footsteps. Now, in a prison, that doesn't seem very unusual, but they were heading our direction. They weren't Lijin's or Taku's or Jay's guard's, I'd memorized them. These were different. A kid's. Maybe a bit older than us. Actually, once I listened closer, they were the combined sound of several kid's footsteps.

I spun around right in time to catch them stopping a few feet away from our table. They all had smug looks on their faces.

"What do you low-lifers want?" Jay yelled at them, annoyed.

"Revenge, pipsqueak," the male that seemed to be the leader or alpha of the little group responded.

"Revenge? Seriously? Nobody here has ever seen you. Scurry along and go crawl back into the hole that you crawled out of," Rowan told him.

The boy flipped back his hair like he was showing off. It was almost as if he thought he looked cool. It was disgusting, though.

"I wasn't talking to you, idiot. And I'm talking about the girl." He could have meant me or Lexi, but the way that his eyes bored down into me made me think that there was only one possibility of who he meant.

"I don't know you," I clarified. But, he just ignored my statement.

"I'm speakin' for the world when I say this: you deserve what's comin' for you," he said.

"But I haven't done anything," I responded.

"Shut it, Mist," a tall girl with long bleached-blonde hair and blue eyes snapped. She looked like a life-sized Barbie doll.

Mist? I was puzzled over the name she had used. *What kind of name...-?*

The alpha boy stepped forward and, before I could register that he had moved during my thoughts, slashed his fist across my face. I fell out of my chair from the unexpected impact and slammed my head on the cold and hard tiled floor.

"Hey!!" Jay and Rowan hollered, standing up quickly and shoving their chairs backwards. They screeched loudly.

I propped myself up on my elbows. The boy kicked my chest, thrusting me back down onto the floor before I could do anything about it. Then he clawed at my face, cutting it with his nails. I had to do something.

This was something that I really didn't want to deal with right now. Not with everything that had happened last night. I kicked his thigh, the highest thing I could reach from where I was when he stood up in egotistic triumph. He stumbled back for a second, but then grabbed my ankle and pulled me into the air, putting his face into mine. Honestly, I was impressed that he could hold me so high without struggling. At least, without showing me he was struggling. I was now upside down and my hair fell as well as my shirt. I crossed my arms, pinning the fabric in place.

Ever since that day, that wretched day, when I had been transported to the LEFP, every time that I got into a fight I would lose all sense of... everything. My sight, my hearing, I wouldn't even be able to feel my body. And then, when everything would come back, me and whoever I was squaring off with were usually both pinned to the ground by guards, but it would be pretty obvious that I'd won. I couldn't put a reason behind what happened. There was no explanation as far as I was concerned. But, it never failed. It was every single time.

"This'll feel good," the boy spat, preparing to turn me into a human piñata. He seemed really happy to be able to hurt me. I was surprised no guards were here yet. But, that actually would play out in my favor.

"Dido."

"...?" That caught him off-guard. So I smiled. My movements weren't my own. But this time, unlike all others, I was kept awake and aware to experience it all go down.

I grabbed his throat and punched his nose, letting my shirt fall for the split second that happened before I was dropped down to the floor once again. I hit my head again, everything flashing white for a moment. It took a second for me to shake off the pain before I was able to jump up. Jumping into the air, I spun, letting my foot travel towards the side of his head at a high speed. He tried to dodge, but he was *way* too slow and my foot collided with his nose. That knocked him back. His nose started to bleed and it enraged him. He shot forward, thinking he could take me out. He was embarrassed to be getting knocked around by someone three quarters of his height and about three or four years younger and wanted to prove himself to everyone watching. I easily blocked his fist and then swept his legs out from under him. He came down heavily, hitting the tiles with a lot more force than I expected.

Then a sharp pain tore at my left arm.

"*Ack!!*" My body came back into my control and I gripped my arm, digging my nails into it, trying to numb the pain. My palm began to burn and I swear that I saw the white fabric of my sleeve start to singe in several little spots all across it, up to my shoulder. The boy in front of me saw my drop in concentration and took the opportunity to punch my face. I felt the skin around my eye give in. The pain erupted in bursts that throbbed.

Finally, *finally*, the guards made their move. "6519!" one of them shouted. "QUIT IT!" They grabbed the boy and pinned him down. He snarled several curses at me, vexed that he'd been stopped, but I couldn't stop thinking about my arm. A guard grabbed my shoulders and pushed me to my knees. Something that I noticed was that the guard atop of the boy was holding his wrists while the one on me held my shoulders instead. Was it just the way that this certain guard stopped fights or did it have to do with the fact that it was me who he was pinning down?

"Who started it?" the guard holding me down demanded. His voice shook more than it should have. I could have been being paranoid, but what if...he was scared of me as well? I looked down at the ground in thought.

"Him," Rowan, Jay, and Lexi all responded together. I could sense the indecision in the guard before he asked the other, "Do we punish them both?" What? It was clear protocol that all participants in the fight were punished, depending on how they fought back. I had fought harder than he did, so, according to their rules, I would have been sent to my room for a longer time period plus any other punishment that the guard decided upon. It didn't matter who started it. Eventually, the other guard just shook his head and I was released. But I didn't move. I remained sitting on my knees. I had always wondered what really happened that made me lose all of my senses. But what if...what if...there was something...inside of me? It sounds crazy, but it fits. Maybe it takes control when I get into fights. It could have done something that I wasn't aware of which would have brought others to the conclusion that I was dangerous. It'd explain the looks, it'd explain the hatred. It would even explain the alpha boy's motive of 'revenge'. But this just surfaced more questions that doubted that, so I decided that I was being overdramatic.

But, as I looked down at my burnt sleeve, I couldn't help but wonder if I was close.

The guards took the boy away. Then, while I still sat on my knees, the bleached blonde girl crouched in front of me. The way that she sat made it very obvious that she had too large of an ego.

"I'm Arabi Tencan. The most badass person in this facility. You are an embarrassment and a freak. To lose so badly to someone like him? Ha! Pitiful." Had she *seen* the fight? "You will realize how many people here are thousands of times better than you, like me, if it's the last thing you do," she whispered with bold–too bold–intention.

I bared my teeth at her, not enjoying this one sided conversation from Barbie with a big and preppy self-image. She scoffed and then stood up and waltzed away. Everyone else in their little group followed her. After a moment, I felt Rowan's hands on my right arm, urging me to get up as well. Jay touched my left.

"Xan, let's–OUCH!!" He retracted his hand and shook it madly. "Your arm! It's so...*hot!!*" I didn't hear him. I just kept looking at my sleeve while Rowan and Jay argued over whether or not Jay was overreacting.

Do they know? Is that why their hearts race? Is something going to happen to either the LEFP or me? Is that why Lijin seemed so preoccupied?

"D-do I have something inside of me?" The words slipped out before I could stop them. Rowan stiffened on my arm and Jay sucked in a hushed gasp.

"Wh-what makes you ask?" Rowan stuttered. Avoiding my question with a question. It was absolutely suspicious. Sussy baka. He couldn't have sounded any more startled that I'd think about that even if he tried.

"That would be weird. I don't know what you're talking about. There's nothing inside of you, Xan," Jay told me. Now, his answer was more calm and believable. But, his pulse wasn't normal. They helped me stand once Jay figured out how to hold my arm and not get burned.

"It was just...a hunch," I replied to Rowan's question. He nodded and we took our seats at the table.

"Are you alright?" Lexi questioned, twirling her hair around on her fingertips to calm her anxiety. I wanted to respond, but I couldn't help but think about my estimate. "Mist". That's what Arabi had called me. Maybe I could ask a guard. But who would respond? Lijin wouldn't tell me. Jay and Rowan wouldn't keep anything from me unless they were told to. And they didn't listen to many people. I remembered seeing Lijin with the boys in between my blackouts which meant that he knew what they did. Which meant that he was the one who had ordered them to be quiet.

I wonder...instead of going through the hassle of explaining myself to a guard, I might be able to ask someone else–

"Xan?!"

"Y-yes?" I snapped back into the cafeteria. Everyone around me had faces full of worry and concern.

"Are you sure you're–" Rowan started.

"I-I'm fine, really," I reassured him. I got to relearn that the universe was against me when, ironically, my head throbbed painfully and the vision in my left eye went blurry. "*Agh!*" I shoved my hand up to hold my head.

"You should go see the nurse," Jay commented.

"No, I-I'll be fine," I protested. They ignored me.

"I shall report to your guard the location to find you at," Lexi said.

"You really don't have to–"

"Nonsense." She stood up. Taking one second to quickly take a look at my subject number, Lexi bowed to each of us and then left the cafeteria. The boys at the table stood up, also, prepared to escort me, so I unwillingly joined them.

They walked me to the nurse's office which was also on Ground Level. It wasn't very big and it was empty besides the nurse, Miss Beighley. Nurse Beighley was a short and plump woman with brown hair that was always pulled up into a messy bun. She had rectangular glasses that framed her features nicely. She wore navy blue scrubs that had several pockets on them with the LEFP's logo. Nurse Beighley was kind and caring, but had reactions to everything that she emphasized and didn't even bother to try to hide.

When she saw me, she gasped loudly.

"Oh my goodness!! What happened to *you?!*" she cried. See? No filter. I didn't even look that screwed up, and she knew it. And I came here a lot. She was just making a scene.

"I got in a fight, what's it to you?" I replied, kinda annoyed for some reason. I clamped my mouth shut so that I couldn't be rude again. I couldn't say the wrong thing if I didn't speak at all.

"Oh, uh, well...l-let me help you, dear." She coaxed me over to take a seat on a long white examination table where she told Jay and Rowan to sit down across the room in blue plastic chairs before she wiped my eye with alcohol wipes and cleaned off all the blood. I watched her, uncomfortable with how close she was to me. Lijin came in a few minutes later and, seeing that the nurse was busy, he walked over to stand by the boys. Nurse Beighley made a face at my wound when she was finished cleaning it for some reason, but she tried to hide it by smiling at me before she turned and waved Lijin over to her, acting like she didn't do anything.

"It's remarkable," she whispered. Barely audible, but my ears picked up every word. "She came in needing stitches, but the bleeding stopped quickly and it's already almost healed."

Lijin nodded, not seeming surprised *at all* which made him look really suspicious. I narrowed my eyes. "Thanks, Beighley. I'll take it from here." He turned to us. "Jay, Rowan, Xan, let's go." I gladly got up and left, the walls starting to feel a bit too close together.

We were halfway up the stairs when he finally spoke, asking, "Did you guys eat?" I shook my head and then we all took turns responding.

"No."

"Nuh-uh."

"Nope."

He sighed. "I'll figure out a way to take you to go eat a little bit later." There was a pause. I decided to cut through it and intercept the silence.

"Lijin?" I asked. He watched where we were going, making sure we didn't run into anyone.

"Hmm?"

"How come my eye healed so quickly?"

"...!" That caught him off-guard. He stumbled on his footing and almost fell down the steps. He clearly didn't notice that I had heard the conversation about my injury. Honestly, that kind of shocked me. Lijin knew very well that I had good hearing. He must have just been too focused on what Nurse Beighley had been saying. "Th-they, uh, p-put something in the new alcohol wipes that helps speed up the healing process. You know, tech and medicine these days. The things they can do." His blood streamed in quick pumps.

"Bullcrap!" I exclaimed. "Nurse Beighley was surprised by my recovery." I crossed my arms. Jay and Rowan watched the scene in interest.

"Y-you heard?"

"I hear everything." I stared into his face, watching the nervous sweat that rolled down his skin as he swallowed hard, at a loss for words.

"Well...I-I'll tell you later, okay?" he proposed.

"...*Really?*" I asked, suspicious.

"Yeah. Really."

"Fine. If you say so." We made it to my room and an idea hit me. If Lijin wouldn't tell me what was going on, then maybe someone else could. I couldn't talk to any guards because Lijin was the only one that I trusted. So who would be the person that Teraki would talk to about these kinds of things? If he knew a lot about this or who 'Mist' was, then he would've told someone. Right? He'd been my guard for almost four years. That's too long for him to not mention anything to someone. I decided to make an excuse to leave. "You guys go on in. I have something to do. Don't worry. It isn't dangerous or anything. I'll be right back." They looked at me in question and then each other. My guard responded first.

"Be careful," Lijin warned. "And don't be too long."

"Yup." I let them all go into the room and then waved as I closed the door behind them. Then I headed down to a small office on Ground Level I knew of that was "birded"–in Rowan's words–by guards. But I'd figure out *something*. I had a plan in mind. It couldn't be *that hard* to swoon and deceive a couple of guards.

I'll figure out Lijin's caretaker and ask them everything they know about 'Mist'. Find out what Lijin himself won't tell me.

I wanted to know what I was. And no matter what, I was going to figure it out.

getting away
it's something that we think is easy
until we try
i've thought about it since childhood
and i still will when i die
i tell myself it's unneeded
though, deep down, i know otherwise
the thought is like an open cage
that cuts my wings when i try to fly
the words without the promise
is like a horse without its knight
and the hope without the temptation
is like a warrior without a fight
something dark stirs within me
and i'm not quite sure why
i think of myself as a star
shining in solitude in the abyss of the night sky

–PRISONER JOURNAL OF

SUBJECT 3029

Eleventh   3029

I found my way to the small office and avoided being seen by any guards until I was able to enter cautiously. I shut the blurred-glass door and turned to the desk before I swung my arms up and then down in triumph with my hands in fists, mouthing, "Yes!" And then, spoiling my celebration, a presence emitted from outside, so I sighed and opened the door back up again. A female guard stood with her hand outstretched, ready to open the door. She pulled it back to her when she realized that she now didn't have to.

"Can I help you?" I asked when she didn't speak. She brushed her fingers on her uniform and stood up straighter to reevaluate herself. She cleared her throat.

"You aren't allowed in there," she stated firmly.

"My guard told me to grab something for him," I lied with fluent persuasion.

"I didn't hear anything about a prisoner being sent down. Who's your guard?" she questioned, hands on hips and eyebrows raised. I read her name tag. 'I. Whosivitch'. Unusual last name, but alright.

"Lijin Teraki," I told her. I turned to shut the door and leave her behind. "Now if you'll excuse me–"

"Teraki, you say?" I rolled my eyes in annoyance and spun back around to face her. She had her arms crossed as she leaned against the door frame. So unprofessional. "What are you supposed to be getting?"

"His guardian's number."

"Wouldn't he have...WAIT." Recognition flashed across her face. *Here we go.* "If you're Lijin's, then you're...!" She looked at my hand in shock and disgust. I pulled it behind me, wanting to cry all of a sudden at her reaction. Even though I'd seen that same reaction 700,000 times. The woman who I now didn't like took a step away from me. "You're the Raq kid!!" She said it like it was an insult.

"Yes," I said, growing peevish by the second. "And you're the ugly Whosivitch woman. Oh-no!! Crazy, ain't it, princess?" She faltered back another step. This woman was clearly afraid of me. She knew the exact thing that I was here to figure out. But of course I couldn't ask her. She wouldn't tell me. "I would like to get what I was told. And stop judging people by the events that they don't know of!!" I snapped. As I shut the door, I made a note to myself:

Emotions were intensified when visited and turned hard to calm down. So I needed to be careful with how I felt towards things.

I took a deep breath and tried to forget about my outrage.

I scanned each drawer, looking at the floor number. It only took a few seconds to find the 7th floor. I pulled it open and looked through the tags on the files. They were in alphabetical order by last name, so I found Lijin in the lower half. I pulled out his file and laid it down on the desk. The old and crisp folder fell heavily onto the wood. I sat in the leather chair and opened the paper.

The first thing I saw was a photo of Lijin stapled to a contract that had him agreeing to become a guard; no matter who his subject became. Then, flipping through, I found a document about his persona and history. It had his age, date of birth, phone number, email, criminal record–which was clean, by the way–, address, full name, and some other crap that I didn't really care for.

Then I found what I was looking for.

'Current and Past Guardians'

"*Lotaría.*" The word left my lips in triumph. I didn't really hear it myself. I wasn't focused on it. I didn't think anything of it. That was a mistake, of course. I should have.

The ones at the top were his current guardians. There was one name listed. I scrambled through the drawers of the desk until I found a document of probably something important. I tore a piece off of it since I only needed a small amount and I made that my paper. I found a pen and gripped it in my left hand and started copying down the person's name, age, address, and phone number. I mean, why not have it all? I was already here, why not take what was provided? I shoved the paper into my pocket when I finished and then looked at the file.

To my shock, there were a total of six names listed as guardians. *Six.*

Meilynn S. Teraki. She was his only current parent.

Lanten D. Teraki. He seemed to be married to Meilynn. It, uhm, also said that he was deceased. In big red letters, too. Harsh. They were really emphasizing the fact that he was dead. I scowled and then moved on to the name under that.

Alicia A. R–

The door burst open. I looked up with a start. Several full-fledged guards filed into the room, surrounding me. I clenched my jaw, aggravated that I had been so consumed in Lijin's file that I didn't hear them coming. But I kept a calm appearance.

"3029, thee shall pay for thou actions," a heavy voice boomed. I recognized the weird speech pattern of a person who was literally just trying to be special and different with the way they talked. I knew who it was immediately.

"This seems completely unnecessary, Galry. It's called *research.* Ever heard of it?" I closed the file.

"Thee are trespassing." He took a step forward, trying to intimidate me. I couldn't see his eyes because of the visor on his helmet. Galry wasn't a personal guard. He was one of the ones who kept people in line.

"Thy rests thy case," I said, leaning back in the chair. His hand fell for his gun. He pulled it out of its holster.

"I shall do what mean be necessary," Galry warned. He meant to seem menacing, but the sight of the pistol just spiked hot adrenaline into my veins and thrilled me. I leaned forward, sliding my hands on the desk and slipping my left foot slightly to the side, preparing to launch myself away from the gunfire. He took that as a denial to my reasoning so he cocked the gun, loading one of the bullets.

The side of my mouth slid up into a grin. "DO IT. I dare you."

"Do not push me, child." He pointed the pistol's barrel between my eyes. I giggled, feeling more daring than usual. This was always how I acted around Lijin. Brave and stupid. Walking the tightrope between games and punishment. But with other guards? I usually tried to avoid doing that. I didn't care for any guards besides Teraki. And now, was I really about to get shot at? Was I really hoping to?

I-I think I was.

"Don't tell me what to do, old man. I'll push your buttons all I want. Push, push. Poke, poke." Fire flashed when his finger put pressure against the trigger. A loud bang rang out. I flinched deeply, but tried to move past the instinct and I leaned slightly to the side. Something gold and shiny spun through the air trailing smoke. It moved slowly while everything else froze. It was like I was watching a movie scene play out in slow motion. I watched it graze my cheek as a high pitched whine pierced my ear. The bullet slammed into the shelf behind me. Papers exploded and a small streak of blood sprayed from my cheek.

Then things moved normally. Every other guard drew their gun.

"Strike 1," I said. A chorus of '*chick-chick*'s echoed throughout the room. Now everyone was ready to shoot at me. Great.

"*Den tha to ékana an ímoun sti thési sou,*" something muttered. I scanned the room for the speaker, but found no one who fit the raspy threat. I started to get queasy. Nobody in the room had said anything. Who had spoken, then? I couldn't understand what they had said. Nor could I tell what the language was. I heard someone move so I spun back around, ready to flee if the situation proved necessary. But they weren't getting closer to me. They were *backing away*. Sweat ran down their faces and each heart pumped faster than the last. They were practically shaking in their boots as they gripped their guns harder.

"*THE SEAL?!?!*" one of the guards shrieked, his face pale. *The what?*

"*I aimatochysía gínetai efkola.*" For some stupidly crazy reason, I somehow understood one of the words. '*Aimatochysía*'. The word meant 'bloodshed'. *Who the heck is talking?* I wondered.

Then the anonymous voice barked the order, "*Skýpse!!*" I understood it as 'DUCK DOWN!' or 'BEND DOWN!' which meant the same thing in this case, so I shoved my body to the floor just as several bullets rocketed into the cabinets behind where my head originally was. And then, as everything progressed, I started to understand more and more of what the voice was saying.

"*Roll to the right!*" it commanded in its foreign language. I did as I was told as the left side of the desk was washed over with bullet holes. I flipped my hair out of my face to watch dust float away from the desk, thinking about how I could've looked like Swiss cheese. *Whoa.*

"*Now forward!*" I somersaulted to the floor in front of me as a guard slid around the opposite corner of the wooden desk and shot at where my body had laid moments ago. In awe, I cheered, "Hah-hah!!" The voice had helped me evade death. Dodge the bullets. It was able to tell me when and where the guards' next moves would be and how I could avoid them. Wasn't that just a teeny tiny bit...awesome?

This strange new voice seemed reliable and suspicious at the same time. I still couldn't figure out who they were or what language they spoke or how I understood them when all I knew was English. But that was the least of my worries at the moment.

"*Slide to your left and grab the scissors that were knocked off the desk in the ruckus. They should be on the floor.*" I did as they said and waited for my next instructions as the group of guards shifted around, half of them not wanting to even get close to me and the other half trying to figure out how to put a golden bullet in my skin. "*Let this guy shoot. He shall miss and then you stab him. Then run.*"

"What guy?" I whispered. But, sure enough, a guard standing by the door pulled his index finger towards him. The bullet flew right past me when I didn't move. I shot up in time to see and dodge another bullet that was aimed directly at me. I managed to make it to the man before he even knew what was happening–before any of them knew what was happening, actually–and I shoved the scissors into his shoulder, causing him to swing his arm in pain and shoot the ceiling light. It shattered and the glass shards struck several people, causing a louder commotion. I weaved my way around him and out the door in the middle of the chaos. I slammed it shut and then hastened away from the scene.

I found a dark corner under a set of stairs and behind a stone pillar. I leaned my back up against it and let out all of the air that I didn't know I was holding, suddenly panting and exhausted. Then I had a split moment of panic and scrambled to check my pocket for the paper. I sighed in relief. It was still there. *Thank God.*

"Congratulations, you didn't die," the voice told me. I couldn't help but look around me, scanning for anyone, *anyone*, that could have said that. But, I was alone. Greeeat. Creeeeepy.

"C-can I ask one question?" I whispered, attempting to communicate with it.

"...?" I took the breath as a sign that they were letting me speak.

"Who are you? *Where* are you? How come I can understand you? W-what language do you speak?" The more things I asked, the more things I wanted answered.

"*That is more than one question.*"

"I-I realized. But who are you? Th-that's my top question." I stuttered. "...And why did you save me?"

"*If you die, I die. And I speak Greek, imbecile. You understand me because it makes things easier. That's how it works.*"

I stared off into space, just listening to the words that floated around me from nowhere in particular. None of this made sense. And yet, it all fit my suspicion. Maybe...–and you can laugh at me–but maybe...the thing talking was inside me. In my head. I was its host and if the host dies, the inhabitant goes down with it. Right? That would fit its words. But God, how I hoped that I had just gone insane.

"*I am not to be disrespected. I am K–*" They went silent and my arm burst into agony. I screeched as I spat out the newly flowing blood from my mouth. I fell to my knees as the overwhelming pain consumed my entire left half. Blood dripped down my arm and hand onto the floor, staining my sleeve and glove. I bit back another scream, staring at my left hand. The skin on my lip broke and my teeth dug deeper, but stopping now would give way to all of the screams that were caged in my mouth and chest. All were sounds that would surely burst my eardrums.

My arm grew hot so I had to let go of it. My sleeve started to singe until one of the tiny sparks lit up and caught fire. Before my eyes, the fabric turned to ash and fell to the floor in one great sweep of the flames. The metal clasp on the cuff melted. What was causing this insane heat?!

"...?!"

Then I saw it, just for a second. Purple bands like ribbons ran up past my shoulder, weaving back and forth, overlapping each other as they traveled up my skin. In between the gaps were different symbols. A birdcage, a shattered heart, a skull, a knife, an eye, and–

And then it retracted painfully into my glove, abruptly. With the end of the experience, my vision blurred. Everything swayed as my body began to collapse and fall over, the strength leaving my limbs. I did everything I could to keep a firm grip on my consciousness. I wanted to stay awake. I wanted to know more. I couldn't pass out now! I still had to go back to Lijin, Rowan, and Jay! I still had to know who had been talking to me. I still wanted answers. But I failed. My consciousness managed to slip out of my grasp.

"Darn it!!" I murmured as the cold tile pressed up against my cheek. Everything faded away. *Darn it!!*

● ● ●

"She-she's not...dead...is she?" was the very first thing I heard when I started to come back around. I couldn't open my eyes immediately. They were too heavy. But I could still feel my body ache.

"No, retard, she's not dead! She's just knocked out."

I shot up, terrified that whoever had found me could see my arm. The images. The ribbons. The mark. One of the people screamed and fell back while the other simply just pushed his body away. I turned my body into a defensive stance with my left arm positioned behind me. It throbbed, causing me to grimace.

"Hey, you're alive!" My eyes focused on the speaker. After everything rocked and went blurry for a second, things cleared and I was able to find Rowan on the floor. Jay stared at him in question before he turned back to me.

"What were you doing down here that you passed out? Are you okay? And what happened to your sleeve?" he asked. The series of questions made me revisit what had happened. He'd mentioned my sleeve. I glanced down at the arm still behind my back. My pale skin was clear all the way down to my glove, which relieved me. All I could see of my mark was the blue lines on my fingers. Nothing more. I was quite surprised that the glove had even survived, though it was stained red. The dried blood ran down my entire arm and the floor beside me looked like a freaking crime scene. There was the melted clasp, the fried sleeve, the blood from my arm, and the blood that I had spit up. The amount of blood was outrageous, but it made another thought come to mind. I touched my cheek. No slit. No blood. The cut from the bullet had already healed.

"What's up with my regeneration level?" I whispered to myself. I must have waited too long to respond to Jay because Rowan began to speak.

"We heard gunshots," he explained, not hearing my inquiry, "so we came down to see what happened. Your, uh, state made us think you'd been shot. But we saw no bullet wounds."

"I wasn't shot. Their aim was horrendous," I muttered. *And someone helped me.* But I still couldn't figure out who. They had been about to tell me when...my stupid mark extended...And when it spoke, one of the guards had cried, "*THE SEAL?!?!*" 'Seal'. Like to keep something inside of something else. To trap something.

"*If you die, I die,*" it had said.

Someone's hand touched me. I jerked away, lost in my own thoughts and confused that I had been pulled back out of them.

"Xan..." Lijin touched my left arm. I stepped back, pulling it from him. Why would he touch me?

"Stop." The word left my lips as my feet faltered and I fell slightly, catching my balance mid-fall. Everything spun in circles. An emotion welled up in me and all I could do was question it. Scared? Not me. Never. Mad? All the time. And yet...

What...what am I?!

I wanted to be angry—if I had to be anything. But, instead, I was just scared. What was going on? What had happened? And why did my stupid 'host' theory fit?

"I'm sorry," I told them, losing my cool. I needed to get out. I couldn't breathe. I was spiraling. I couldn't take this. *Whose voice did I hear?!* I shook my head, clearing away the thought. *No. I-I don't want to know!*

I shouldn't have been so freaking stupid. I literally could have just pushed Lijin till he snapped. He would've told me eventually. Just like he'd said. It would've been easier to just believe him and wait it out. I wouldn't have gone into the office. The guards wouldn't have attacked me. I wouldn't have heard the stupid voice. And I wouldn't be spiraling like this.

Everything spun, my brain's connection to my eyes and body glitching out from all of the stress that I fell into. My feet staggered in placement. I was going to pass out again. I was sure of it.

Then someone's arm wrapped around me and pulled me into them. Their hand held my head to their chest, forcing me to pay attention to them. I could hear their heartbeat in my ears. The sound was somehow soothing.

"Calm down, Xan or you'll pass out again."

I closed my eyes and forced my breathing to a steady rhythm.

"I don't know what happened or why you're freaking out, but forget it. It's okay. You're safe," he told me. My lips parted before I considered the words.

"I don't feel it..." *Shut up!!* I screamed at myself.

"..." He didn't respond. I seemed to have stumped him. He didn't know how to continue. I pulled away to look at him. Lijin stared at me, his blue eyes filled deep with an invasive emotion that I couldn't exactly locate or put a finger on what it was. His lips opened, like he had something to say, but I cut him off.

"I didn't mean to say that. I never mean to do or say...*anything*. Nothing's secret anymore." They were true words, but I didn't like that I was already sharing them. They were meant for just me. Nobody else was supposed to hear them. *Oh my God, just stop talking!!* "I-I have to go." I pulled from him and started to head away from the situation. I couldn't deal with it. I made eye contact with Jay and Rowan and the concern on their faces stung.

"I-I'm fine..." I whispered to them. Though, I was far from it. I couldn't bring myself to believe the words. And it was clear that they couldn't either. But they stayed silent nonetheless and I was able to scurry away like a mouse that knows it's met its end.

Pathetic, I thought as I focused on my toes as they hit the metal stairs. And I swear, I heard a deep voice laugh slightly. A shiver coursed through my spine and my arm throbbed.

Only when my door clicked shut did I feel sick. My stomach churned and contracted and I propped my body up against the wall. Since I hadn't eaten or drank anything, there was nothing for me to throw up, but the feeling of my insides being ready to turn inside out was anything but pleasant. The gagging stopped and I made my way to my bed. I sat down heavily and the rustle of paper in my pocket reminded me of what I had been doing.

I opened up the paper to look at it. Then I looked around me. *Where am I going to find a phone?* I sighed. I'd have to either ask for Lijin's or take it. How could I seriously not think that I'd need a phone to make a phone call? What the heck had been going through my head?

I grunted at the pain in my muscles when I stood up. I walked across the room to the wooden desk. I got down on my knees and pushed the stool away to reveal a cardboard box. I lifted the lid and pulled out an off-white folded piece of fabric. I stood and set it down on top of the desk so that my hands would be free. I then unbuttoned the front of my shirt and undid the clasp on my right wrist. The cloth slid down my arms until I held it in my hands.

The mutilated shirt was placed back in the box while I placed the other on my slim figure. I buttoned it over my bra and stomach, leaving the top button open to leave room around my throat and ensure I didn't suffocate–Rowan complains about that one. (It's always Rowan when it comes to stupid stuff like that)

I kicked the stool back into place and sat back down on my bed, sighing. I still had so many questions that I didn't have answers to.

What am I going to do about that voice?

"*Not kill it, hopefully.*"

My senses spiked and my spine straightened. I scanned the room, coming to the much despised conclusion that I was still alone. I picked a spot on the wall across from me and stared at it, spacing out so that I could focus on the words the voice used. I pursed my lips together.

"You're back?"

"*I do not have much time. It'll close the gap that I found. But, yes. For now.*" What's '*it*'? I wanted to question. But I kept focused.

"Are you going to finally tell me who you are?" I asked.

"*Ha. Impatient, are you? Yes. I will. But I've decided to ask you first,*" they responded. So they didn't even know who I was? I wasn't sure how to feel about that.

"No, I asked first. Answer me before you get cut off again." My insides twisted and tightened at the thought of their answer. I didn't want to know. I really didn't. But it'd keep me awake at night if I didn't figure it out. I mean, if they were the mysterious 'Mist' character, then there'd be no point in stealing Lijin's phone. It'd just be so much easier. And I might not ever get a chance like this again. So I dove in headstrong.

"*To be honest, I am quite surprised that you do not know who I am. Child, be careful with how your tongue moves with me. Watch your words.*" I swallowed and they chuckled with harshly frightening prep for their name.

"*I am Kakó, the Dragon Of The Mist, the 2nd Great Terror.*"

My little sisters have decided that my becoming a guard was to become closer to her. I guess. But they can't guess at the intensity behind why.

Samrinn thinks that I have a crush on her. Eww. I'm 12 years older than her. I have no love interest at the moment. I'll make that much clear.

Litz believes that her and I both had a secret friendship for a few years before she was born and that I wanted to restore that. Her and her silly fantasies.

There's much more pain involved than that.

–GUARD JOURNAL OF

SERGEANT 7560

twelfth   1863

The tension in the room was so thick you could cut it with a knife. Me and Rowan were sitting in uncomfortable chairs in a small room while Lijin was deeper in the two room interrogation chamber.

I didn't quite understand what they were talking to him about, but I had decided beforehand that I didn't want to leave him. So, here we were. Confined to chairs while Xan's guard was asked random questions that I couldn't hear. It made me nervous, not knowing what was really happening.

Rowan was sweating and honestly looked a bit green. I could tell why and didn't blame him. I felt the exact same way.

We had been discussing whether or not we should go try to find Xan since she had been gone for around half an hour when we heard gunshots. We ran down to Ground Level, curious, when we found her behind a pillar. Her body was crumbled up in an unnatural position and the floor was stained with blood. I remember how my heart had dropped.

Rowan had froze and I swallowed my breakfast as I knelt down beside her to check for a pulse. The blood in the veins at her wrist thumped encouragingly under my index and middle fingers. Rowan had stuttered with a pale face, asking if she was dead. I buried the fear I shared with him and told him she was just knocked out. Then, he had stepped closer and she shot up without warning, spooking the both of us. I just pushed my body away while Rowan screamed.

She had been so...childlike. And not in a good way. She seemed so frightened. She looked ready to either burst into tears or fall apart at any moment. And that was *not* the Xan we knew.

"Do you think they're asking him about Mist?" Rowan whispered, drawing me back in.

"He's probably getting scolded for letting her wander alone," I responded.

"...Or both." The subject was clearly making him uncomfortable and fidgety, making his leg bounce up and down with anxiety. I kicked his shin, causing him to stop, whirl, and give me his 'what-the-heck' face. I reluctantly let the side of my mouth curve upwards into half of a grin.

"Don't worry. I have a plan," I told him.

"You do?" The pain and worry in his voice stung.

"Yes," I admitted, nodding. Just then the door on the wall beside us opened. Lijin stepped out, his face stone-hard–unusual for him. Me and Rowan stood up together. The guard that came out next was tall and bulky.

"Teraki–" the man started.

"I know," Lijin replied, clearly irritated. He turned to us and motioned for the door. As we left, he started to swear under his breath, angry. Rowan cocked his head to the side.

"Uhh, you okay?" he asked. Lijin just sighed heavily.

"Yeah."

"Sure don't look like it," I murmured. He changed the subject, pulling away from the topic.

"I'm working on the ritual thing and...I think we're gonna go for it," he announced. *What?!* I asked myself.

"Go for what? Having it at that lady's house?" I listened intently as they talked, still kinda shocked.

"Yeah. I just need to figure out how to get you guys out of here."

I couldn't help but laugh. They turned to me in question. "Done," I said. "Got it all laid out." Both of their jaws dropped, which I found entertaining, but they quickly righted themselves. "Lijin, I have officially decided that we're breaking out. Tonight."

● ● ●

I was on the floor of my room revising my plan in my head. I mapped out the layout of the LEFP and started to keep a list of all of the shift hours of all the guards I could think of. Then, from my window, a faint 'meow' hit my ears. I sat still, completely sure that my brain had processed something wrong. But then I heard it again. The sound of a cat. I got up and walked to the window. The sun was still high in the sky and casted faint shadows on the bars in the sill. And in the depths of one of those shadows was a small animal, sitting upright, staring at me. Its coat was a smokey gray and its eyes a bright green.

It licked its paw and then took a hesitant step forward. I turned to look at the door to make sure my guard wasn't about to burst into the room and then clucked my tongue and stepped back, inviting it in. It jumped down from the window and landed on the floor. It was very scrawny, that's for sure.

I moved forward and it jumped back, arching its spine and hissing at me. I took a step to the side, saying, "Calm down. It's okay." as I sat down on my bed. After a moment, it followed and hopped up beside me. I stuck out my hand to let it have my scent and then, when they seemed comfortable with me, I scratched the top of their head until the cat began to purr.

"I don't know how you got up here. I'm on the second story. And I'm not sure how you plan to get down," I spoke aloud. It meowed again. Then it looked at the window and shivered. I crossed my legs and let it take its time as it crawled into my lap. It curled up into a ball after a moment's hesitation. I brushed my fingers across its back, leaning backwards.

"Well, I guess it's safe to assume you aren't leaving. Especially not anytime soon." The purring was ruptured with a sneeze that I laughed at. "The thing that I least expected to do this afternoon was talk to a cat." Since it had its back to me I had to look at its build. I observed it closely to find that it was a girl because of the slightly less bulky way that a female cat's bone structure was designed.

The smokey color of her coat reminded me of smoke from...a fire.

I swallowed what rose in my mind and throat and moved on with my thoughts.

Maybe I could name her something that somehow relates to fire. Like Flicker, Sparky, Match, or even Smokey. But, as I tried to find a good fitting name, something else entirely rose to mind. The name hurt, but it was one of the most meaningful names to me. It referred to one of the most special things that I used to have.

"What do you say?" I asked the cat. "How about Rhekkun?" Her purrs grew stronger and she rubbed her head up against my heel. There was no way that she could actually understand me, but it had to be a sign. She was supposed to be named Rhekkun.

Something spilled from my right eye. And then my left which was hidden behind my bangs. I wiped the water away in anger, frustrated that my feelings were betraying me. A flame lit inside me that I had desperately put out a long time ago. It licked away at my lungs, burning my insides and making it hard to breathe.

Then I stomped on the flame until it flickered out.

The irony of it is pitiful. You'll see soon enough.

I'm leaving this crap-hole and you can't stop me. I know that you, Taku, read my journal when I go to sleep so I'll just have to tear this out to leave to you since I plan on taking the notebook. Well, I guess this'll be my final goodbye to you, good sir. We are going to fix Xan. And I am NOT coming back. Ever.

Good luck trying to find me after you read this. I'll be long gone.

Goodbye LEFP.

I'm off to start a new life. And not...kill my family off this time.

–PRISONER JOURNAL OF
SUBJECT 5742

Thirteenth 7560

Jay had given me specific instructions. I was on the course to fulfill them. On my way to Innkuro's room on Floor 9, actually. I didn't expect her to be there, though, she should've been with her subject at this time of day. I was probably the only one who wasn't. I knocked on the door on the off chance that she was there and, with no invitation, I turned the knob and pulled.

When I closed the door behind me, I flipped on the lamp. With the light on, I noticed how her desk was filled with papers with drawings on them. The drawings looked like something only a creepy stalker could create. They were *all* of me and her. I gagged. I then left the desk and crept over to her bed. I dropped down onto my hands and knees and pulled out a solid-black book bag from underneath the bed frame. It was waterproof with two netted side pockets, a zipper in front, two deep zipper pockets, adjustable straps with buckles that would clasp over the wearer's chest, and buckles on the bottom for extra luggage. Something all guards are given at the start of their journey as a sergeant. Now I had two. I sighed. I needed four.

Next, I dug around the heavily unorganized room until I found her pistol. Luckily, beside it were the cases of bullets, all of which I stashed into the bag. Then it was her wireless headset that I took from her. I held it up to make sure it seemed completely intact before I pushed it down into the inside of the bag I was holding.

Footsteps echoed outside in the hallway. I scrambled to shut off the light before the person noticed it was on and then I held my breath, pressing myself into the comforting shadow of one of the corners. Someone knocked on the door.

So it's not Innkuro. That gave me some sort of comfort.

"Innkuro?" a female voice called from outside. *Kayree?* I thought. She was Innkuro's best friend. Another guard. "Are you in there?" *No,* I revised. *Too...demanding.* I didn't really speak with Kayree, but I knew her voice from meetings and such. This wasn't her. "Whosivitch, don't tell me you're with your snotty brat of a prisoner!" That confirmed it. Definitely NOT Kayree. The woman outside grumbled in utter disapproval before she stomped away, annoyed.

I stood still for a minute or two, keeping my gaze fixed on the shadows from outside that I could see spilling in from underneath the door. I waited, just in case she came back or someone else walked by. Eventually, the coast seemed clear. No more people.

Silently, I slipped out of Innkuro's room with the bag slung over my shoulder.

After making the long walk to my own room and shoving the bag under my bed, I walked back up several floors to Jay's guard's room. I knocked, got no answer, went in, and grabbed his bag, gun, bullets, and headset. I was about to leave when I found a small First Aid Kit which I swiped on the off chance we'd need it. Then I slipped out with no interruption whatsoever. I placed everything under my bed with the rest of the stash and then started for Taku's room, which was on Floor 7 with me.

This could've gone better.

Taku was twenty-three years older than me and I was subordinate to him. He had higher authority and getting caught stealing from someone else's room would cost me. Especially if it was him that I was stealing from.

I tapped my knuckles on the bronze door. There was no answer. I tried once more.

"Taku?" I asked, wishing to be more careful than I was with the other two invasions. When no reply reached my ears, I knocked one more time, just to be sure, but nobody responded. So I gripped the knob and rotated my wrist, pulling the door out towards me. Then I walked in and shut it behind my back.

I was reaching for the light switch when a high-pitched alarm rang out. *Crap.* I turned to leave, thinking I could just find someone else to get supplies from. Steel bars sprang out from the walls and clamped together in front of me, blocking the door and my way out.

"...!" *What the hell?!*

I frantically scanned the room, searching for the alarm panel. I groaned when I spotted it on the opposite side of the room...

...on the ceiling. *Now why would you put it there?*

I stepped forward and my foot sank a fraction of an inch below the flooring. Hatches on the walls opened and shot knives. I flipped to the space in front of me where a clicking sound told me to keep my guard up. I was able to drop to the floor as a hatchet tied to a string of steel chains dropped from a compartment in the ceiling and barely surpassed my nose until it swung up into a different compartment that closed and seamlessly blended into the surrounding ceiling, seemingly disappearing.

The whole room's rigged?!

I spun my head around, looking for the gun and headset until I located both of them. I leapt for the gun, but skidded to a halt when a freaking *bowling ball* fell from the space above me and crashed into the space in front of me, splitting the floor and sending fragments of wood flying. I reached over the ball, grabbing the pistol and bullet cases and thrusting both into some of my empty pockets.

Then I lurched for the headset. As I ran, I saw the fishing line below me, so I jumped over it, just to trigger a second one hidden amongst the shadow of the first.

Seriously?! I whined to myself. Sharp throwing needles danced through the air as I tried to dodge them all, still panicking about the siren that was starting to drill a fried hole in the 'hearing function' part of my brain. I reached the communication device and shoved it into one of my back pockets.

Next, I jumped over other trap triggers that I could just barely see and hopped on top of the bed, reaching up as far as I could until I punched in the random code that made the most sense and—thank the Lord of mercy—the alarm shut off. I then grabbed the bag that was under the thing I was standing on and raced to the door. The bars retracted and I gripped the handle—

—when I felt the vibrations of heavy footsteps headed my way. Taku.

Cgah!!...Dang it!!

I rushed back over to the bed and thrust my body under it. The quilt on top hung over the edges far enough that he wouldn't be able to see me unless he dropped down to the ground. I watched, horrified, as the door swung open and slammed against the wall as two black boots stomped in. It was like a game of Hide 'N Seek...with two adults...and one of them had murderous intent.

The boots stood in place—most likely scanning the room. Then they ran to the bathroom, thrusting open the shower curtain. While they were in there, I pulled something off my belt with one hand, then stuck it up to my mouth to grip a small metal piece between my teeth. Guards were taught at the beginning of their training how to easily set these things off by placing them in their teeth and pulling in the right direction. The wrong direction could yank your teeth clean out, but that's okay. I was in distress and had to do this quickly. I didn't have time to worry about that risk. So, I yanked and then tossed it into the middle of the room. The smoke bomb went off, hissing dark blue clouds of smoke everywhere. Taku grunted, trying to find me in the blinding haze. But I shot out from under the bed and out the door.

Fortunately, Taku's room was just forty-eight doors from mine. I ran past rooms quickly, bounding through the hallway, and before he could even find the door handle, I was safe with my door shut behind me. My heart beat so flipping fast, I thought it might explode.

"A lot of work for a backpack," I muttered. Then I sighed and turned back around to carry Taku's items to Rowan. But my hand stopped right before the knob. It was shaking so badly I couldn't even wrap my fingers around the handle and I couldn't stop it.

I had never done anything like this before. Not this extreme. I wasn't this type of person. I didn't steal and I didn't go against the law. It's just how I was. It was the person my parents had raised me to be. Then I remembered *why* I was doing all of this sketchy crap and I clenched my hand into a fist.

Suck it up. You'll be doing a lot of both tonight. It's who you are now. There's nothing you can do about it now. Choosing not to do any of this will get Xan killed. You have no choice. I stopped thinking to myself like a psycho whose only friends were mirrors and stuff and forced my hand to grip the doorknob. Then I left and headed down to the 5th floor.

I watched my shoes as I walked and looked at no one, keeping my head held down. I didn't feel like making eye contact with anyone when I knew very well that I was betraying them all by helping three prisoners escape.

Taku was not at his post when I reached room 5742. I wonder why. I rolled my eyes and then knocked. My knuckles were starting to get sore. A 16-year-old boy with long red-orange bangs and bright brown eyes opened it. He stared up at me. I looked around us to make sure no one was watching when I stepped inside.

"Here," I said, slinging the bag off my shoulder and tossing it to him.

"Whose is it?" Rowan asked.

"Taku's." He raised his eyebrows in surprise as he started to dig through the main compartment of the bag, examining its contents.

"A gun?" he questioned.

"Yeah. Just...don't shoot anyone. Not yet, anyway," I told him. The kid nodded with slight disappointment. "Fill it with things you need. Only necessities. I'll cover the food."

"Got it."

I smiled. Then told him not to take too long. Then I left, got Jay's guard's stuff, and trekked *all the way* down to Jay's room on Floor 1. I was dragging my feet, tired.

The guard slumped on the ground in front of his door didn't notice me until I spoke to him, announcing my presence.

"Hey, Ivan," I greeted, trying to act like I hadn't just broken into this guy's room and ransacked his belongings. He jumped, startled, and then clumsily stumbled to his feet.

"L-Lijin. What are you doing here?" Ivan asked.

"I need to have a small chat with 1863."

He seemed surprised at my response. "W-what about? Why? What'd he do?"

"Oh, he didn't do anything, he's not in trouble. He was, uh, with me when the gun shots went off earlier when the prisoner got into the office on Ground Level. I was going to tell him what had happened." I shrugged. "Just thought he might want to know." While I was in the interrogation chamber, most of the other guards had gotten the news that a subject was on their own downstairs, so everyone knew a bit about the matter. I used that common ground to help back up my excuse.

"Wait, wasn't it your–"

"I need to talk to Rivereay," I cut him off.

"...Oh, uh...I guess...g-go on in," he stuttered.

"Thanks." I opened the door and closed it once I was within the boundaries of Jay's room. He was on his bed, facing me. He must've heard my conversation with Ivan and knew that I was coming. He had nothing in his hands, but I noticed the smell right away.

"Where is it?" I asked. Jay sighed. I grinned.

"You noticed her?" he replied.

"I have a pretty good nose. And one of my...sisters...has one," I explained, sitting down on the floor. The smell of the animal was coming from under his bed, so I reached my hand out towards it, calling, "Here, kitty kitty." A small gray cat ran out to me. She hesitated, stopping when she got close. I kept my arm outstretched, waiting patiently while she smelled my hand. Eventually, she let me lightly comb her body with my fingertips.

"Does she have a name?"

He hesitated and then responded with, "Rhekkun."

"Nice. When did she show up? And, uh...how? Have you noticed how high up we are?" Rhekkun began to purr, rubbing her head against my hand.

"Yes, I noticed! I ain't that stupid! And she showed up a few minutes ago at my window. Now, moving away from the cat, have you gotten the bags yet?" I pulled the bag off my shoulder and threw it to him. Jay caught it and then unzipped it, making sure I had gotten the pistol, bullets, and headset. I smiled.

"Your batch was easy. Rowan's, on the other hand, about got me killed. I had a heck of a time with that one," I stated firmly.

"Wouldn't be much of a loss besides the fact that we would no longer have access to the unparalleled knowledge you possess. We kinda need that," was his comeback.

"Gee, thanks. I feel so valuable."

"Wasn't a compliment."

"Wasn't admission."

He scowled at my quick response. Then he put on the headset. I already had mine on. It coiled around his ear like a hearing-aid. The communication device was actually designed to mimic one so that nobody would suspect anything.

"Range?" Jaymon questioned.

"One hundred-forty-three and a half miles," I replied.

"Wow. Power?"

"Should last a few weeks. Most guards don't really wear them, so three to four weeks would be my guess if they're fully charged."

"That'll work." He turned the earpiece on and then pressed two of his fingers to his ear. That was what would allow him to talk and everyone else to hear him. Jay opened his mouth to speak when a blast of sound exploded from the small devices inside our heads.

"*YO, HOW DO YOU KNOW IF IT'S ON? YOU GUYS HEAR ME?*"

"YES!!" Jay yelled, infuriated as he rubbed the side of his temple. The sound rattled inside my skull and my vision vibrated ever so slightly as my ear started to ring. "Turn down your volume, doofus!" There was a pause.

"*HOW?*"

"The silver knob on the back of it, Samrish. Turn it down. *Way* down," I instructed, the ringing getting louder. After a second, Rowan tried again.

"*Heh-heh. Found it. This better?*" he asked, clearly embarrassed by the way he laughed.

"YES. Thank you," Jay grumbled.

"*Sorry.*"

I shook my head, only to have things spin more. "I think he damaged something," I said, concerned. Jay just waved his hand at me, pushing the topic away and not even acknowledging my words.

"Rowan?" Jaymon asked into the communication device.

"*Yes, Sir?*"

"Has your part been completed?" Rhekkun climbed up into my lap. She watched Jay as I stroked her. The small cat seemed deeply interested in him.

"*Yeah. I got done just a bit before Lijin gave me my stuff. It didn't take me very long, but it should all be completed to your liking.*"

"Good." He picked up his fingers, removing them from the center of his ear so that his voice wouldn't catch in the microphone and play through the headsets. He turned his attention to me. "You should probably inform Xan if you haven't already. I know I haven't said anything to her and neither has Rowan."

"I, uh, have one more thing to do first," I informed him.

"I would get on with it." He turned to look out the window at the slowly oranging sky. "Night fall will come quicker than you'd expect it to." I nodded, then remembered the cat that was still in my lap.

"Rhekkun can come, too." Something small cracked across his face. I think it might have been a smile. Who knows with this kid? Maybe it was. He called to her and she left me then jumped up into his crossed legs. I stood and, for a second, I just watched the boy in front of me as he played softly with the cat. Then I left.

3014, I reminded myself as I made my way up to the third floor.

After a short walk, I found myself face to face with a very tall female guard. I must've still been disoriented from all of the running around because I didn't immediately recognize the woman. She kinda looked like someone I knew...Someone who...was fond of me, but I found obnoxious and–oh wait.

DANG IT, I almost screamed out loud. *Why is it always her?!*

"Hi," I sighed. One word, people. One. Word. And her entire face flushed red! I mean, come on.

"Oh, T-Teraki. You came to see me? It isn't very...private here. Why don't...you and I...go up to my room?" Innkuro asked.

1. Leave me alone with her and I will DIE!

And 2. I had just raided her room.

So it was a definite no.

"Lexi Widler?" I questioned, gesturing to the room behind her. She glanced at the door before gazing back at me.

"Yeah. Why? We can ditch her. She's only, like, six. The toddler will be fine without me for just a bit. You and I can just...slip away for a little."

"You're misreading me. I came to see her. Not you."

"..." She seemed taken aback. I smiled. Then clamped my lips back over my teeth, telling myself to be kind. *But whyyy though?* I sighed. Innkuro was my only way to Lexi at the moment, and since I needed to see the girl, I had to suck it up.

"Can I go in?"

"...Yeah. Sure...Why not...?" The smile on her face creeped me out, so I pushed past her to enter the room. The young girl with short curly hair was laying on the floor, drawing on torn pieces of paper from her journal. She looked up at me, stunned that I would enter her room.

"Hello, Lexi," I said. Her eyebrows knitted together

"Do I know you?"

"Yes. I'm–"

"Teraki," Lexi cut me off, reading my name tag. She sat up. "You are Xan's guard, are you not?"

After Xan had gotten in a fight in the cafeteria, it was this strange girl who had come to find and tell me that she was in the nurse's office because of her busted eye. She had informed me that she was just someone who slightly trusted Xan as a comrade when I asked if they were friends. I had seen this child once for just a brief moment and now I was willing to place trust in her. I didn't know what it was. There was just something about her.

"Yes. I sure am."

"Hmm. What brought you here? What is it that you are needing?"

"Help." Her eyes lit up. She was interested. I had her hooked. "Lexi, this is really important. Can I trust you?"

"Is it for Xan?"

"Yeah. She-she's dying. She just doesn't know it yet."

"...?!"

I continued, "And I need your help to save her."

The side of her mouth curled up into a grin. The child straightened her spine, now sitting a few inches taller.

"At your service, Sergeant Teraki," she told me. "What actions do you require I pursue?"

● ● ●

I knocked. No answer. So I turned the knob and entered without permission. She was on her bed, facing the wall, staring at nothing in particular. Her left hand was cuffed in her right as her nails dug into the glove.

"Xandralin," I said. Her eyes snapped to me and she let go of her hand as if she didn't want me to notice that she had been holding it so hard. Even though I already had.

"Lijin..." she whispered.

"I have something for you." I lowered the bag off my shoulder. Xan watched my movements as I pulled out the headset. I took a step towards her and held it out. She took it, hesitantly.

"Put it in your ear," I ordered. She did as instructed. I showed her how to turn it on. She powered it up and then waited for what I had to say next. "She's in," I said with my fingers pressed to my ear.

"*Nice. I finished my part.*"

"*I'm done, too.*"

"Jay and Rowan...have it also?" Xan asked. I nodded.

"To talk to them, press two of your fingers to the center piece in your ear. It enables the microphone. We might have to adjust your volume, though." She eyed me suspiciously as she brought up her index and middle fingers to her right ear.

"Can you guys hear me?" It came through on mine and I was able to pick up on the note of distress in her voice. What was that from?

"*All clear here, Xan,*" Rowan replied.

"*Seconded,*" Jay added.

"It came through on mine, as well. Though, let's make your volume a tad louder." I showed her how to fix it and then I pointed to the book bag. "Okay. Inside is a gun and bullets. Do *not* shoot anyone unless the situation proves absolutely necessary. Fill the bag...as if...I don't know, as if we were leaving and not coming back."

"We're running away?"

"Why would w-we do that?" My stutter is probably what gave me away. She continued to ask questions.

"When do we leave?" I sighed and she giggled with effort that I don't think I was supposed to notice.

"Tonight. When the sun sets. And after the bell rings for curfew. That's when we leave." The sun was already turning the sky red. The day was flying fast. It was almost time.

Jay's plan was thoroughly designed and worked in theory...but would it actually get us out? I had no idea, to be honest. I mean, it was designed by a 16-year-old. Getting caught would get all three kids punished, me fired, and Xan killed. Staying would also get Xan killed. Neither option was acceptable.

"Meet us in Jay's room fifteen minutes after the bell rings, got it?" I asked, handing her the black book bag. She took it and set it on the bed beside her.

"...Got it."

We smiled together. Then her's faltered.

"Uhm, Lijin? What motivated you to suddenly decide to break us out?" Xan questioned.

"...?" For some idiotic reason, I hadn't counted on her asking that. Which meant I had no answer. Then, when I gathered myself, I let the shock fade from my face to be replaced by a gentle smile that I had seen so many times on a specific person.

"I'll tell you later." It was the same lame excuse that I had used earlier when she had asked me about her regeneration speed.

"You've already played that card," she muttered, catching on.

"Maybe it's the same card. You never know." I started for the door. I still had a few things to take care of. I had to grab all of the necessities that they simply could not get because they were prisoners. Perks of being a guard!

I wrapped my fingers around the handle and then turned back to Xan.

"This'll be fun," I told her.

"You don't know how long I've waited for this. So let the fun begin."

unchained

when my limbs flow with blood
and my heart roams free
looking back at my younger self
it brings great shame to me
for how in terms of power
i was then so weak
hushed lips curse and speak of a name
that brings gods to their knees
it's funny, is it not,
how that name is the one of me?

–PRISONER JOURNAL OF

SUBJECT 3029

fourteenth   3029

BADARA-BRIING!!

Curfew. It was 10:00 pm. Let the countdown begin.

I had packed everything I needed and washed my glove. At the moment, I was standing at my desk with the picture frame in my hand. The photograph of my parents was something that I kinda wanted to leave behind. The last time that I had seen them was when they had come to see me and couldn't even look me in the eye without caution. I was scared of myself...it would have helped to have parents who were fine with *whatever* I was. Of course, I didn't get that. It wouldn't seem logical if I had. Too easy. Only the most important thing ever to me, but that didn't matter. Yeah right.

Flashes of the day they had willingly handed me over to the LEFP hit me like stones. The stones tore through my heart, ripping my breath away. I had to hold onto the frame tighter to refrain from dropping it.

"*It'd make you stronger if you killed them off,*" Kakó muttered, returning.

"No." I took a step backwards. "No, no, no! Leave!"

"*I'd help you. On your own, they see you as a freak, but combined, we'd be someone they kneel to. We can kill your parents and then–*"

"Stop!!" I screamed. The picture fell, the glass shattering as I plugged my ears, trying not to hear him. I squeezed my eyes shut.

"*That won't work. I am in you. You cannot shut me up. Child, listen. They gave you up. They are terrified of you. You'd be better off dead in their eyes.*"

"SHUT UP!" I shrieked. My left arm throbbed, shushing him for the moment. I fell to my knees from the pain. Once it passed, I looked at the broken frame, ignoring my panting and the sweat running down my back.

Is he right? Do they really see me that way? N-no. They're my mother and father. Why would they...? But I had an impenetrable feeling that he was right. I was just a freaky monster to them. All because of Kakó, most likely.

He had told me that he was something called the Dragon Of The Mist. He explained about a man named Kanobi and something about the Vault of Eternal Darkness, yadda yadda. And then how he had escaped, but got himself put in a vessel. Then my mark had spread and he had gone silent. The pain wasn't as bad when he just talked compared to when he did something. Still hurt, though.

I picked up the picture out of all the glass shards. With the frame still around it, it had some weight, which meant that it would carry if I threw it.

My hand twitched, considering the action. I had gotten no support throughout my entire lifetime from them and I was their *daughter*...And yet, I had told them otherwise. They acted surprised, but what if they had always felt that way? They just needed me to say it out loud. What if it was all an act?

They wouldn't even touch me. And they forgot about me for seven years. I couldn't deal with this.

Staring at the picture lit a fire of rage inside me. The rage transferred to my shoulder, then to my arm and hand.

"*Rhagk!!*" I threw the photo at the wall, letting the entire frame shatter and explode. The wall dented. Dust fell from the gash as metal and leftover glass sprayed everywhere. The small pieces flew back far enough to cut me, but I made no note of the slowly dripping streaks of blood on my skin. They'd heal soon anyway.

I revisited the countdown in my head.

~10:07~

I let the slits heal as I searched through my bag for a small box. When I found it, I popped one of the things inside it into my left ear. Turning it on, I found a song and let it play. There was a strange sensation that I got when I listened to things on this. Like something was pouring inside me and neutralizing the pain. I thought it was just because I tended to like music and it soothed me.

I couldn't have been further off.

~10:13~

I shut off the music, putting the earbud and music box back into my bag before I slung it over my shoulder. I took one last look around my room to make sure I didn't forget anything and then ran to Jay's as quickly and quietly as possible. His guard was asleep on the ground. I reached for the door when something wrapped around my ankle.

"...?"

"You'd seriously think I fell asleep?" the guard asked. I noticed that I had not heard a pulse from him. Maybe I just wasn't paying enough attention.

"Uh, yes, I actually did," I stated.

"What are you up to? And where'd you get that bag?" he asked, tightening his grip around my leg. I grasped for an answer.

"I'm...starting a book club. And, uh, *Hobby Lobby*." I tried to shake my leg free. This was embarrassing and a waste of time. I wanted out of this place and I couldn't leave if I was being held down by a guard. And this man did not seem ready to let me be. But then the door opened.

"Ivan, let her in. I asked her to come," Jay demanded.

"It's past curfew, though—"

"I do not care. Let go." The guard let go of me with dissatisfaction and I stepped inside, thanking Jay. He nodded, then cursed at the guard before closing the door behind me. Lijin and Rowan sat on the bed. Lijin stood at the sight of me. He carried a coiled sheet that was just a bit longer than the bottom of my book bag. They each had one on their backs.

"Turn," he said, so I spun. He clipped the sheet to the bottom of my bag. Then he took a step back to face me.

"How did you two get in?" I asked.

"I have my ways," Rowan responded. Teraki stayed silent.

"You guys ready?" Lijin asked us all instead as Rowan and Jay made sure they had everything. I looked at them and they gazed back at me. I was filled with a warmth that blew away any doubts I had about the operation. I smiled.

"Ready," we said together.

~10:19~

"Alright," Lijin whispered. We were behind a stone pillar around the corner from the main hallway. "They start rotating night-shift guards at 10:20. It usually takes until around 11:00 to get everyone fully swapped. That means we have forty minutes to get out of here. This hallway has tons of guards in dips and shadows. There is a right turn at the end and then the main doors. The main doors are guarded heavily and they will shoot at us if we're caught. That means you guys have to be sly and fast. Understand?" We chided with quiet affirmatives. "Now, is everyone clear on the plan?"

Whaaat did I miss?

"Yes."

"Got it down."

"I-I totally missed something. There's a plan?" I asked, confused.

"You don't need the plan. Just stick with me," Lijin replied. I scowled. The time hit 10:20 and guards started to swap places for the night.

Some seemed stern and on alert while others joked lightly amongst themselves. Fools.

Lijin started to sweat. Rowan looked excited. Jay looked...normal.

"*Have fun with it, child.*"

"...!" My left temple throbbed and I grabbed my head.

Rowan turned to me. "You alright?" he whispered. It took a second for the pain to pass, but when it did, I waved my hand at his question.

"Y-yeah. A-all good here." He didn't buy it. Figured. He placed his hand lightly on my shoulder.

"You'd tell us if something was going on, right?" Rowan asked. I almost responded with the fact that I could ask them the same question. But, instead, I just nodded.

"*This night shall spare lots of bloodshed. Mmm. Delicious,*" Kakó murmured in my ears.

"Shut up," I told him under my breath.

"What'd you say?" Jay questioned.

"Nothing. When do we leave?"

"Here in just a moment, Xan. Be patient." He stared straight ahead. A few seconds went by and then his eyes narrowed. Then they sprang back to their original size. "Now!!" Lijin exclaimed right as the fire alarm went off. The sound pierced my ears, setting off my immediate instinct to cover them. Since I hadn't been expecting the alarm, I shut my eyes instead of moving like I was told to. Lijin grabbed my arm as he and the boys ran.

The guards transferring out of their shift ran towards the cause of the sound.

"It's 3014!" one of them yelled. The sound traveled through the flesh of my hands. Then the realization hit. I knew that number.

"...!" I opened my eyes and uncovered my ears. I looked back towards the source of the high-pitched howl. Just as I'd expected. Sitting on the railing like I had the other night was a small girl with short curly brown hair. Her eyes met my gaze in the chaos. She smiled.

"Find freedom." I'm not sure how the words reached me. It was so loud. But I heard them. And they sank in deep.

"See you out there, Lexi." Her grin widened, though I couldn't tell if she could hear me or if she was just happy. Then, guards ran up the stairs towards her so she spun to fight them off, tearing her eyes away from my own. A small piece of me seemed to fly away with her. Some guards noticed us. Jay smiled slightly.

A gray blur raced out from nowhere in particular and clawed at their legs. As the guards battled with the anonymous creature, Lijin pulled us all into a small spot where the wall dipped in for a guard's post. He scanned the area and then pulled something off his belt, popped a small metal ring off, and then tossed it out in front of us into the hallway. It exploded and started to hiss a dark blue fog everywhere. I let my eyes narrow in on what was beyond the haze and quickly came to the conclusion that no guards could see us. The gray creature bounded up to us. Before I could panic, I realized that it was a cat. It rubbed its body up against Jay's legs and he bent down to scratch its ears.

"You have a cat?!" Rowan and I exclaimed together.

"Shh!" We went quiet. "Details later. C'mon, Rhekkun, we're first." He motioned for the cat to follow him and it did. Jay ran forward and then leapt off the ground onto the wall where he pushed his body into a spin and grabbed a guard by the collar, knocking him out when he landed, throwing him into the ground. He took the man's pistol and shot at the wall ahead of us, causing all guards to drop down. Rowan shot forward. Jay tossed him the pistol as he ran by. Lijin pulled me with him. We dashed through the haze. The cloud was starting to fade and I could see silhouettes of guards getting closer. Rowan shot at something on the ceiling behind us and it rained throwing needles. Several guards were pierced by them.

Then we had to deal with the guards *in front* of us.

Jay's cat–Rhekkun, I think he called it–picked up speed and attacked the two closest guards. Lijin pulled out his own gun and a grenade. He tossed the grenade into the air and shot at it in midair. It exploded, knocking a grand total of five guards to the ground.

At this point, the fire alarm had shut off and had been replaced by an escapee siren.

"TERAKI!" someone yelled.

"...?" Lijin spun, but didn't stop running. I turned with him, curious.

"Oh," I muttered. It was just that Whosivitch woman from the office again. I was uninterested, but Lijin hesitated for a moment at the sight of her.

"Innkuro..." he whispered. She didn't pursue us. She just stood there, her hands over her chest. Something flickered inside of Lijin. Not love. Not grief. But remembrance. Recognition. He stopped running and the color drained from his face. His heart thundered with an irregular pattern in my ears. Rowan and Jay spun around to see what was going on.

"Hey, Lijin?!" Rowan yelled over the siren. "What's wrong?!"

"We have to continue moving!!" Jay reminded us. I tugged on Lijin's hand, trying to get him to move.

"R-right. I-I'm fine. Sorry, Xan. Let's go." He turned his back to Innkuro and we resumed our escape.

Higher-ranking guards showed up and I was worried we'd be stopped, but the three boys I was with seemed to anticipate their every move. Hidden traps lurked everywhere and were purposely set off with pin-point timing. One of the three would create some type of diversion, drawing all attention to themselves while the others would either set off a trap or knock guards out manually.

We turned the corner and the main doors came into sight. Several full-fledged guards blocked the exit. Lijin pulled us into a large divot before any of us were spotted.

"This is going to be a bit trickier," he announced quietly. "These guys are tougher than they look. Jaymon, Rowan, you both remember what to do?" They both nodded as Jay placed his cat on his shoulders. "Good. On my signal."

I had no idea what was going on. I looked to Rowan for further instruction, but he was focused on Lijin, waiting for the signal. Jay was the same. I sighed. I didn't even know what the signal was.

We just stood there for a second, listening to the chaos we had caused as my anxiety started to climb up my throat. Then Lijin's hand went up with its first two fingers raised. He flicked them forward and Rowan and Jay sprinted from our spot in the wall.

"Here," Lijin dropped the pistol in my hands and ran after them, leaving me, which made me feel like crying. I was about to yell that I couldn't use a gun when Kakó stepped in.

"*Place your eye up to the top, and then hold it out in front of you with your arms straight. Hold it with both hands, keeping its weight balanced. Load it by pulling back the sliding part on the top of it all the way until it clicks and then letting it swing forward. You might have to push it. Then shoot. Keep your other eye open when aligning it and make sure your target is in the center of your vision.*" I did as he instructed, ignoring the slight pain in my head and arm. I pulled the trigger and flinched against the recoil and sound.

My ears were starting to hurt.

My first bullet hit the ceiling and disappeared, but when I tried again, it hit one of the guards in the shoulder. They collapsed, trying to stifle the bleeding. The other guards drew their guns and shot at us as I began to run. I swayed and dodged, not one hitting me. There were so many gun shots that I couldn't tell who was even shooting anymore.

When we reached the door, Jay, Rowan, and Lijin attacked the guards with some taekwondo looking stuff. I found a guard and made my way over to him before I was noticed and slapped my palms over his ears, making his eardrums burst. His blood flowed out from the sides of his head, but I removed my hands quickly so my glove wouldn't stain.

Lijin swiped his ID card on the scanner next to the doors and they made a '*c-click*' sound as they unlocked.

"Hurry!" Lijin yelled to us, but no one was even thinking about doing anything but that. They ran out ahead of me and I was finally–finally!– about to step outside the doors of the LEFP when a cold hand gripped my wrist. It held me in place. It held me in place in the prison, keeping me from leaving.

"...!!" I spun to see who it was. My stomach dropped.

"Hello again, pest," the woman spat. It was her. It was the woman from this morning. She was back. I hadn't heard her come up behind me. My hearing must've been jacked up due to all of the ruckus. "Looks like you started a riot. Congratulations." She smiled and her lips stretched up too far to be considered normal for a human. "Since all I told you about me was that I'm classified, I guess that you deserve my name." I tried to pull away, but she just squeezed harder. "Doctor Qinglee. Remember it. Oh, and, remember this, too: no one has ever heard my name and lived to spread it."

"...!" The pistol slid out of my hand and hit the ground.

Before I could move or respond, Dr. Qinglee reached up and poked my forehead. My sight was clouded with some type of visions. No. Actually, they were memories. Fragments of memories. My memories.

My parents giving me up.

Galry slamming me into the table with Rowan and Jay.

The stares.

People spreading rumors about me.

Me being alone.

The stares.

Guards watching *me* more than anyone else.

People freaking out when I got close.

The stares, the stares, the stares!

I yanked my wrist from Qinglee and fell back, hitting my body on the doors, but glad to be out of that dark corner of my mind. She smiled. It was the creepiest freaking thing I had ever seen.

The doors opened back up from the outside. "Xan, c'mon!" Jay yelled at me. I stumbled to find the pistol and then the door, tripping over my own feet, as I watched Qinglee. Sweat rolled down the back of my neck and my heart threatened to explode.

"I'll find you...Enjoy it while it lasts, Xandralin," Dr. Qinglee said. I ran out, not able to look at her anymore. And she let me go.

The LEFP was the largest building in all of Bludriss, our home state. It covered about 140,000 square acres of land, give or take, not including the river that surrounded that. The reason that its size was so large was because the LEFP also owns the gigantic mountains that surround it. Which meant, on foot–like we were–it would take a fairly long time to actually get off the LEFP's property.

But we were determined, and a bit quicker than I thought we'd be. There were quite a few trees which hid us well in the dark. We bounded through them, headed straight East. I took in the gracious feel of the grass and dirt between my toes. I had never been outside before. My parents had never let me leave my room except for the bathroom. The prison had a courtyard, but it had fake grass and was walled off so you couldn't see the horizon. Well, I mean, you still couldn't really see it right now either because it was *so* dark, but you would at dawn.

I couldn't wait for that.

~10:33~

I first noticed him losing pace about five minutes after we had entered the forest. I just assumed he was tired until he slowed A LOT. We all slowed down with him so he could keep with us. Then his eyelids started to sink and he started to trip over his feet. Then he collapsed.

"...!!" "...?!" "...!" We gasped together.

We all stopped to make sure he was okay. To our horror, he absolutely wasn't. He was already laying in a pool of blood. Lijin turned his body over with urgency. In his shoulder was a large blood-stained hole.

"Oh my God!" I cried.

Rowan had been shot and hadn't said anything about it. Now he was unconscious from loss of blood.

Never in my life have I met someone who I would do anything for. Nobody ever truly loved or trusted me, so I decided there was no point in giving what wouldn't be returned. But the peculiar girl whom which I discovered has made me think otherwise. I am not stupid enough to not have put the pieces together after my last journal entry. I have figured out who she is. I have heard the stories about her. But there is one part that I do not agree with.

Xan is not a monster.

She is just tired of being called one.

-PRISONER JOURNAL OF

SUBJECT 3014

fifteenth 1863

"Jay, compress the wound! Xan, help me find a knife and a lighter!" Lijin ordered us as he began to dig through his bag. It took me a second before I could get my body to move. I was shaking frantically at the sight of *so much* blood. Rowan's entire right sleeve was soaked through. It brought up memories that I preferred to forget.

A young girl, soaked with her own blood, unconscious. I had wrapped her up in my arms, despite the flames around us. Her long blonde braid was burnt and bloodied. My hands, chest, legs, and knees had been consumed by her blood. I had sobbed so hard my chest had seared like crazy.

"*ALICE!!*" I had wailed at the dead body in my hands.

"...aymon!! Jaymon, please!!" Xan shrieked.

"...!" I pulled away from the picture in my head and ran to Rowan. I dropped to my knees and Lijin tossed me a towel. I pressed it to Rowan's shoulder, gradually adding more of my weight. It soaked through in moments. Rhekkun hopped down from atop my book bag and laid down on his chest.

"Rhekkun, off!" I yelled at her, but I was ignored and the cat didn't move. She looked up at me, her pupils wide to see in the dark. She started to purr.

Something hot spilled onto my fingers. I looked down to see how bloody my hands were. He was losing too much blood.

"Lijin!" I called, terrified at the horrible possibility that erupted from the scene. It was so abrupt. H-he was fine just moments ago. I-I couldn't lose him! I lost the cool mask that I fought so hard to keep on. I started to panic as the metal smell of blood filled my nostrils, sending me into sensory overload. Everything spun as my breathing increased dramatically. That just made it worse. I started to relive it. The blood. Her body. All my fault.

Someone's hands pressed against the tops of mine.

"Jay, please stop crying," Xan begged. Tears spilled from her eyes. I became conscious of the fact that they were pouring from my own, too. I was scaring her.

Xan had another towel that she pressed against the bullet wound. Lijin took the lighter and used it to heat up the knife until it was basically smoking from how hot it was.

"I need everyone off," he ordered. Xan and I pulled back and Rhekkun hopped off to lay on the bag that I had thrown off my shoulders. The guard with us pulled the shirt off of Rowan.

He took the tip of the heated knife and pressed it to the front of the wound, attempting to cauterize it. Rowan's flesh sizzled as it burned. The seconds ticked by in slow motion and yet the time lost sped by. One...Two...Three...Four. Lijin removed the knife.

"Turn him over. I need the exit wound." His voice was so calm. So controlled. It was the complete opposite from how I felt, my heart battering around like a bird in a cage desperately trying to escape.

The person who helped Xan roll Rowan over wasn't me. At least, I don't think he was me. There was no way that I could've done that. All I could think about was how low a chance of survival he had. And yet, the hands that moved him were attached to my arms. Maybe it was me.

Lijin did the same thing to the back of the bullet wound, pressing the tip of the heated knife to the skin until it was cauterized.

I found that my numb fingers had found home on the vein at Rowan's wrist as I watched his chest rise and fall.

"Please, Rowan, please," I muttered. He had lost so much blood. I was covered in it. My body still shook painfully and wouldn't stop. Just like Alice. So much like Alice. I hadn't been able to save her.

No, not again. I-I couldn't do it again!!

His heart started losing pace.

"...!!"

"RIVEREAY!" My head snapped up. Xan was holding Rowan's body up as best she could, still silently crying. Lijin was using some type of alcohol from a First Aid Kit to clean his shoulder. "I need you to help Xan hold him up." I scrambled over to lift the limp body further off the ground.

I can't do this. I can't deal with this.

"The bullet wasn't still in him," Lijin whispered to us. "Yes, he lost a lot of blood, but it looks like he might just make the cut." He pulled out a bottle of medicine, dosed it, and poured it into Rowan's mouth. Probably something to help with the pain. Some form of morphine. Me and Xan tilted him back slightly so that it'd go down his throat. Then Lijin wrapped bandages around Rowan and had us lay him back down.

"I'm not a medical sergeant, but in training, they teach us a handful of medical actions. I'm not the best there is, but..." He looked at Rowan for a moment. "...I think he'll be just fine. And," he said, "for good measure..." He pulled out an EpiPen and stuck it into Rowan's thigh.

"What's that gonna do?" Her voice was small.

"It's an adrenaline booster. It'll keep him going for most of the rest of the trip. And hopefully, it'll wake him up faster." She kinda just looked at him until he smiled and told her, "All it'll do is help him heal. He'll be alright."

Xan sighed with relief and fell onto my shoulder. She was still crying, but I could tell how hard she was trying to calm herself down and get quiet. Her hands, glove, shirt, and pants were all stained. I looked down. It was the same for me.

Again. The scene was so similar.

"Jay, you're shaking," Xan told me, sitting up. "H-he's going to be okay."

Of course, I was *so* happy about that, but...he'd been *saved*. Why hadn't she? I had buried this so deep, long ago. This scene, this situation brought it all back. I couldn't bear it.

It had been all my fault. I had...

I buried my face in my arm, sobbing.

They watched me. It was unlike my character, but I couldn't suppress it. Not when it was brought to light like this.

"Jay..."

My past was coming back to me. I didn't want it to. I *really* didn't want it to. My greatest mistake. It was coming back to mock me.

But it was just a mistake. Just a mistake. That's what I had always told myself. And yet Rowan was here. Rowan was going to make it. She hadn't. It had been me. I had done it. It wasn't a mistake. I couldn't call it a goddamn mistake when it was worse. So much worse.

I pulled on my hair and doubled in on myself, wanting to disappear. Wanting it all to disappear. Go away. And wanting her to come back.

Lijin and Xan didn't ask what was wrong and I didn't explain on my own. They most likely thought that it revolved around Rowan. It didn't.

"...*Alice...*" The word slipped out between sobs.

● ● ●

Lijin carried Rowan on his back and Xan carried his bag. We walked in silence. My abnormal breakdown had stopped and I had quit crying like a wuss. We didn't speak of it and I was grateful because I was embarrassed as hell. It wasn't every day that you saw a 16-year-old guy break down in tears over something totally unrelated to the situation.

I'm not quite sure when he finally came around, but after a while, he decided to state his presence.

"Yo, how long have I been dead for?" Rowan asked. It startled me and Lijin when he spoke, but Xan was unfazed.

"You mean, how long have you been *alive* for?!" I snapped.

"Just over ten minutes," Xan responded. I turned to her. Her posture made her appear tired, but she wore her usual grin. Rhekkun ran at her feet.

"You knew?"

"Yeah. His heart rate and breathing pattern changed."

"Yeah, uh, God sent me back. Said I didn't make the cut," Rowan joked, but his voice was forced. He was in pain.

"You've been out for half an hour," Lijin informed him. "Can you move?"

"Which part of me?" He sat up a bit and tried to rotate his shoulder. He winced. I rolled my eyes, hiding my concern.

"He means, 'can you walk?' " Xan said.

"Maybe." Lijin stopped to set him down. Xan gave him his bag and we resumed walking. Rowan was shaky at first and moved a bit slower than the rest of us, so I hung back with him. His shirt was back on, but it still presented a large hole.

"Your face is red," he told me. Then he noticed my clothes. My *very* bloody clothes. "..."

"You lost a lot of blood," I murmured, my eyes fixed on the land in front of us. He looked down at his own outfit. It just about matched mine.

"...Were you...uh...you know,...crying?"

"No!" I scoffed, automatically putting my defenses up high.

Rowan's lips parted, but a distant howl cut him off. The four of us skidded to a halt and slowly turned around–back towards the LEFP.

"Release the bloodhounds," Lijin whispered.

"What?!" Xan questioned in alarm.

"It's past 11:00. They've gotten past the chaos. They're coming. They are releasing the hounds. Those are specially trained dogs used for finding escapees."

"Then we need to move," Rowan said.

"But it's all forest for miles," Xan pointed out. "They aren't finding us anytime soon."

"We have to run roughly fourteen and a half miles," I told her. "Better start moving." Her body drooped at the measurement. Rowan twitched.

"*Fiiine,*" she sighed.

"Great," he muttered.

"Ooh! Maybe we'll find a stream," Xandralin hoped, jerking her feet into motion as we resumed our run. "We could wash our clothes."

"That'd be nice," Lijin agreed. "We might want to be a tad more... presentable when we enter the suburbs."

"Suburbs? Where exactly are we headed?" She skipped forward to be beside him. Apparently, she didn't know where we were going.

"There's a small family taking us in for a few weeks," he explained.

"Only a few weeks?! Are we coming *back*?!"

Me and Rowan just watched.

"Uh, well,...no. Just, uh, we'll figure it out." He sped up; she fell back. Defeat plagued her features. Rowan chuckled. She shot him a look and he shut up. I couldn't help but laugh at Xan's superiority in the situation. She began to laugh with me until she abruptly stopped, grasping at the left side of her face.

"*Uhagk!!*" I could practically see her silhouette throb. She spat up blood. "*G...Go...away...!!*" she grumbled. Her body trembled and then her knees gave out.

"Xan!!" We both reached out for her, but her left side was emanating way too much heat. We couldn't touch her without getting burned. Not from where we were.

"It's always something with you kids!" Lijin commented as he lunged for the girl. He pressed her right side to his own body and sat her on his lap. Her limbs shook and she squeezed her eyes shut.

"...*L-leave...me...alone...!!*" she whimpered.

Does she know? Does she know what's inside of her? Does she know about Mist? Is that who she's talking to?

A faint light danced on her sleeve in the darkness. Her poor shirts, man. At this rate, she wouldn't have any come time of the ritual.

Very hesitantly and very cringy-to-watch-ily, Lijin slid his hand up to rub the top of her head. He seemed worried. *Incredibly* worried. She still shivered, but her body started to calm. When her eyes opened, she burned with anger.

"Argh! I'm fine! I'm not a child!" She pushed away from Lijin and tried to stand, but fell, and then caught her balance on the way down. I knew very well that Xan didn't want to have to depend on others. Rowan and I were the same way. But I did feel like her anger right here was going a bit too far.

"Xan, you need to calm down," Lijin told her.

"No, stop! I'm fine, seriously!" As her rage grew, so did Mist's hold on her. We all just stared, dumbstruck, not sure how to react, as she screamed and crumbled. Her violet eyes stretched wide and shook madly. She forced both hands to her ears.

"EFF OFF, SCREW YOU!! LEAVE ME ALONE!!"

The trees shook and small animals scattered from them. Rhekkun cowered behind my legs. Lijin paused for a moment, doing what looked like remembering something. Then he mumbled and drew a complex cross in the air with his fingertips and then walked up to the girl, knelt down, and poked her forehead. Xan's arms fell, and her eyes drooped almost instantly.

Next, her slim body fell forward.

"Whoa!" Despite his injury, Rowan reached out and grabbed her arm, swinging his body to the ground in front of her so she wouldn't hit the dirt. He sat on his knees with Xan draped over his shoulder.

"W...what'd you do?" she asked, attempting to catch her breath,

"I suppressed it." The dogs howled in the distance. "But it puts a major strain on your body. I won't be able to do it many times. Maybe one or two more at most."

"He's...so...loud..."

I froze. *It talked to her. It really talked to her.* Mist was speaking to its vessel. No wonder she went so crazy! Only God knows what it could've said.

"...I-it speaks to you?" Lijin stammered, clearly as surprised as I was.

"See...I knew you knew him." She slowly stood up. "Just...didn't think ...you'd ever actually admit it"

"…"

"We have to move," I whispered. Rowan looked up at me.

"Yeah. Right." He stumbled to his feet. Then started walking. Lijin stood to follow him. I walked with Xan. Her left arm hung lower and limper than usual and she breathed weirdly. But she kept her body upright and never complained.

"Hey, Jay," Lijin said a few minutes later, "come up here real quick. Rowan, you can go walk with Xan. Okay?"

"Sure. Got it." Rowan and I swapped places.

"What do you want?" I asked, bloody hands in stained pockets.

"How much longer do you think you can hold out?" Lijin whispered.

"A few hours, maybe. Why?"

"Rowan's dragging and the ragitou I used on Xan will knock her out in fifteen minutes at most." He glanced back at them.

"The what?"

"The ragitou," he said, like it was obvious.

"What in the heck is a ragitou?"

"It's like a…well…I don't know; you read, it's like a jutsu."

"Seriously? A…jutsu?" I raised my eyebrows, suspicious, though I couldn't tell if he could see me. I don't think he could.

"Sorta. There's countless different types. Special people can use special ones. That's one of the only ones I know. My mom taught me. The one that I used just suppressed most of the energy in her body, forcing Mist back inside."

"Your mom seemed to know a lot about the Dragon Of The Mist," I pointed out to him.

"Yeah, well...Anyway, if they fall asleep, do you think that you could carry Xan a little ways if I carry Rowan?" It was an odd question, but considering her weight–well, all of our weights–because of the amount of food we were served, I'd probably be able to hold her for a little while.

"I guess," I told the guard. I turned back to look at Rowan and Xan. They laughed together, chattering lightly.

"Not all night," he clarified. "Just until we find a safe resting place."

"Got it."

"Okay." He pulled his voice back up to its natural volume. "That's all I needed. You can go back now." It sounded like he was smiling, though it was kinda hard to tell. I turned and walked back over to Xan and Rowan. They were both dragging their feet.

"I don't know 'bout you guys, but I'm getting tired," Rowan said.

"That's because you're wounded. You're weak when you're wounded," I told him. I could just barely see him place on a tired smile.

"Hey, I'm not weak! You're wrapped 'round someone else!"

Xan laughed. Rhekkun ran around her to be by me. I bent down and put her on my shoulders. The small cat curled up on top of my bag to watch our surroundings. Every time a hound made a noise, her ears would swipe back and she'd scan the forest. To be honest, it was kind of like Xan in the cafeteria. She was usually able to maintain focus on Rowan and I, but she still did it.

"Guys, there's a stream up ahead. We can dip in it to cover up our scent for a little while," Lijin reported.

" 'K," Xan murmured.

~11:32~

"*Mrow?*" I set Rhekkun down with everything else. Lijin took off all his gear, just leaving his clothes on and then we all stepped into the freezing stream. The cold burned my toes and made my clothes stick to me. Rowan winced when he dunked past his shoulder. As he moved around, he stared at the water, watching it closely. I didn't know why, but I let it be, not saying anything.

We moved to a deeper part where the water was up to our chests.

It had been around ten minutes since Lijin had placed the ragitou on Xan, so he and I both watched her very carefully. I told myself that I was prepared to catch her when she fell, but I knew that it'd still catch me by surprise.

As we washed our clothes off, Xan went underwater, dunking her face and hair.

She didn't come back up.

Memories. The brat doesn't have them. She doesn't remember all that she has done.

Don't worry, dear child.

You will when I'm through with you.

G. Qinglee

–EXPERIMENT JOURNAL OF

SERGEANT 0001

Sixteenth 5742

"*Xan?!*" Jay's voice was filled with panic. I spun around faster than should be legal and/or possible for someone wounded, tired, and in water. Lijin wasn't visible and Jaymon was frantically searching through the water.

"What happened?!" I yelled.

"She went under, but didn't come back up!!" Jay yelled back. Lijin broke the surface, his dark bangs in his eyes as he gasped for air. He had a waterproof flashlight clenched tightly in his hand.

"Are you guys able to go under?!" he called.

"I can't swim!!" Jay responded. I could.

I swiped the flashlight from Lijin and dove underwater. The water was murky with no fish or plant life which was unusual. I spun, creating a full circle, then I swam around that, scanning more area. I searched until my lungs felt ready to burst. I sprang to the surface, gasping for air.

"I don't see–!!" I started to scream with panic when something pulled me under. "*Grph!*" The flashlight was ripped from my hands and I couldn't see anything. Then, with a great burst, everything was visible. Above the water were clouds, trees, and the sun, while below was filled with rocks. Though, I could not find the legs of Lijin and Jay. I swam for the surface anyway, but was stopped in my tracks. It dug something sharp into my ankle and I screamed, losing some of my air.

Then I saw it.

It was a girl.

She had long black and red hair that flowed out everywhere. She had dark, piercing eyes and patches of scales scattered across her ghastly skin. She wore a long shirt and dark gray shorts. Her feet were bare and swishing water away from her body as she pulled herself closer to me. The thing digging into my skin was her fingernails.

She let go of my ankle to grab my shoulders, stabbing her long nails into my bullet wound. When I winced, she smiled. Her lips stretched up far and her teeth were sharply pointed.

Who—no—what the heck is she?! And why is she in a random stream in the middle of nowhere?! And where is Xan?!

The girl put her face up next to mine.

"Stop moving. Bait isn't supposed to fight back," she crowed.

Two things. 1. She had just talked underwater. 2. She had also just called me *bait*. That's a little creepy. Correction, really creepy.

Bait for what? was my first thought in response to what she said.

"Dragons," she said as though she could hear my thoughts. Then she pressed herself closer. She grabbed my shirt.

"You look like some pretty tasty bait," she cooed.

...E-excuse me? What...in the actual–

"Shh. You'll lose all your bubbles." My chest seared and started to close as if on command. I tried to move, but my body froze in response to her touch.

Then, as I neared the last amount of air my half full lungs held, the girl pressed her face to mine and we locked lips. I was surprised and disgusted. My face flushed, despite myself. I pulled my body in the opposite direction, but it wouldn't move.

Then something slammed into the side of the girl's face, knocking her off of me and to the side. Her cheek and eye bled, changing the water's color. And then its visibility. It sloshed back to the original foggy texture.

My body came back into my control and I aimed for the surface, at my limits and not even daring to figure out what had hit her.

Someone grabbed my arm. I was ready to fight her off, but she pulled me to the top of the water. Our heads broke free and we both gagged and sucked in air.

"Rowan!!" Lijin yelled, but I couldn't focus on him. I turned to the person on my arm. The person clinging to my arm for dear life wasn't the creepy girl. It was Xan.

"Get out of the water!!" she shrieked between breaths.

"Xan!" Jay called. Him and Lijin helped pull us out of the stream with them. Once we were on land I scanned the stream. I couldn't see her. It gave me no security.

"Where'd she go?!" I asked, still coughing.

"Who?"

"I don't know!!" Xan responded. "I hit her with a rock. I didn't see what happened to her because I was paying attention to you."

"Slow down, slow down," Lijin intervened. "Who are you guys talking about?"

Xan's eyes never left the water. "It was a girl. She looked about my age. She-she pulled me under the water, but I got away. The water turned, like, clear and I couldn't see any of you. Then she appeared again and she was holding Rowan down. Th-the water, I dunno, kinda moved with me and I was able to get enough momentum to hit her and get her off of him. She could talk underwater and was really strong. And creepy. God, was she creepy."

I remembered the feeling of when she'd kissed me. My face flushed red again.

"Rowan?"

"Ah! Nothing! Yes? What?" I sighed when I realized that they couldn't see me blush in the dark.

"...Uh...anyways...did you recognize the girl?" Lijin asked.

"No." I shook my head. He turned to Xan, but she just mimicked my actions. Then she slumped back onto the ground.

"Xan?!" I panicked.

"Gather your wits, I'm still awake," she told me. "I'm just tired."

"I'm surprised you haven't passed out yet," admitted Jay.

"Same," Lijin said.

"Can't pass out in water. That's how you die," she whispered with her arm over her eyes. My stomach tightened at those words. Death in water was not something new to me. It was actually very old.

I shook away the thought. Then stood up, ignoring the pain in my shoulder.

"C'mon," I told her, extending my hand. "Let's move before she finds us." Xan took my hand and I helped pull her to her feet.

"Right." She took a few steps and then stopped. "What the...? Lijin? What is...?" And then her body slumped.

"Xan?!" I called as I grabbed her before she hit the ground. But there was no response; she was out cold. "Lijin, what–?"

"She's fine. It's expected." He turned to Jay. "You good to carry her?"

"Sure."

"Wait, expected? What does that mean?" I questioned as the girl was transferred from my hands to Jay's back while he slung his bag onto his chest. Rhekkun meowed with disappointment before trotting back to the path.

"I'll explain later," Jaymon told me. Yeesh.

● ● ●

We had officially been walking for three hours and I was so tired, I wanted to cry. My shoulder ached and I was cold. Xan was still on Jay's back, but even he was dragging. Sweat glistened across his neck and he breathed in huffs. She was as tall as him, maybe a bit shorter, but we were all thin and slender so she probably wasn't much weight to carry. But even so, Jay was carrying a fourteen year old girl on his back and he had been for the last two hours.

I opened my mouth to complain about being exhausted when my feet intersected and I fell down.

"*Mmph!*" They stopped.

"Do you need me to carry you?" Lijin whispered with a kind smile.

"No," I said, standing back up. "I'm a big boy, Teraki, I'll be fine. How long until we rest?" Lijin looked around. Then pointed southeast.

"There's a small cave right over there. We can sleep there for the night."

"Oh, thank God," Jay exclaimed before I got a chance to.

"I can still take her," he offered.

"No," Rivereay rejected. I stood still, locking my legs into place and entertaining the thought of just falling asleep where I was.

"C'mon, Rowan. We're so close. You can make it." I groaned at the aching pain in my bullet wound as I jerked my legs back into motion. I wasn't wet anymore which was a plus, but I was still cold and stiff. I hadn't seen or heard anything that indicated that the girl had followed us and, after a while, I ended up giving up looking.

The cave was a small but deep dig under a jut in the hill. It wasn't really tall enough for any of us to stand in, but it was better than nothing. We rolled out the flat but heavily cushioned sheets and I flopped down, relieved to be off my feet. Lijin pulled out a small portable lantern and turned it on, a tiny flame flickering to life inside. Xan was tucked under her sheets and Jay sighed when he laid down beside me.

"Finally," he said sarcastically, "a dirty cave that barely fits the four of us. Hurray."

"Would you rather sleep outside?" Lijin asked him. Jay thought about it, then turned over with a grumble, giving the guard satisfaction. He chuckled. Then he turned serious.

"Okay, here's the deal. We'll sleep here for a few hours." *Only a few?* "It's somewhere around one in the morning so we'll have about five and a half hours until dawn. That should give Xan enough time to come around, Rowan to heal, and all of us to recuperate. Then we'll move again."

"Got it," Jay and I replied together.

"Get some sleep, boys," Lijin told us as he turned out the light. I was asleep in moments.

• • •

They were enclosed in the liquid, unable to breathe. I watched. They gagged, gasping for help as they tore at their throats. Pathetic. My emotions of hatred flooded those of love and reason and the water spiraled up along their necks. I wanted to stop, but I couldn't.

"*No!*" I wanted to scream, recognizing the scene.

But my small fist closed anyway. The water sliced through their throats and then–

I jerked upward, panting. It took me a second to realize that I was still in the cave.

It was a dream. No. That stupid memory.

I looked around, praying I hadn't been screaming. That's when I noticed her empty bed–er, sheets. *Xan?!* I was about to run out looking for her when I saw the pale silhouette against the moon's bright shine. She was sitting at the mouth of our little cave with her knees pulled up to her chest. She just sat there, staring at the stars. Her hair blew out in thin wisps.

Then she pulled her knees closer to her and a silver whisper escaped her lips. "My little window never gave a view quite like this."

"It is pretty, isn't it?" I whispered back. She nodded.

"Even with all the trees...the stars still shine through." She turned to face me. "You should go back to sleep. I'll be back in here in a moment."

"...Okay." I laid back down. "Oh, uh, hey, Xan?"

"Wassup?"

"Don't let it change you."

"...?" She seemed surprised by my words, but before I could give her a chance to ask about them, I was pulled into unconsciousness. This time, without nightmares.

Before I came here, I had 1 person who was really close to me. She was a year younger than I was, but we were inseparable. She looked up to me and I adored her. I'd do anything for her and it was that impulse that killed her. She was my little sister, after all, and to mess with her, you had to mess with me. And like all kids, she got messed with. The entire neighborhood burned and died for it. Including her.

Her name was Alice.

–PRISONER JOURNAL OF

SUBJECT 1863

Seventeenth 3029

I woke up before everyone else. I *had* gone back to sleep after talking to Rowan, but I still managed to wake up an hour before dawn. Eventually, I got tired of being alone, so I got up and walked over to Lijin. He was asleep on his side, snoring softly, when I stomped on his ribcage.

"*Oof!*" He shot up. "What the heck?! What was that for?!"

"Up 'n' at 'em, dweeb!" I chimed.

"You're supposed to be recovering, not rejoicing," Jay groaned, turning over to face away from me.

"I'm still tired," Rowan moaned from beside him.

"Sounds like a you problem, not a me problem! C'mon!"

My stuff had already been packed up, so I was completely ready to keep moving. I knew too well that this wasn't possible, but I wanted to start the day off right. New places to go, things to see, freedom, new critters, thirsty bloodhounds, angry prison guards, a mad scientist who wanted my blood, crazy mutant fish people in streams, absurdly obnoxious demons. Yep. The wonders of nature.

The guys of the group finished packing everything back up. Then we exited the cave. It was not yet dawn, so the sky was still a dark blue.

I had not heard from Kakó since back after the Rowan incident. He was putting more and more nonsense in my head. He had told me about how killing Jay, Rowan, and Lijin would spare me lots of trouble and time. How he and I could run to the city and satisfy our (his) bloodlust. Then he started listing people, what they did, and ways to end them. My mind was filled with images that just made everything worse. Blood. Screams. Horror.

I shook my head, pushing away the thought.

"At least she's energetic again," Rowan shrugged.

"A little *too* energetic if you ask me," muttered Jay.

"Shh!" I hushed. "Now, fourteen and a half miles, yes?"

"In total, correct," Lijin said.

"And we've traveled?"

"About seven and a quarter."

"Which means we're halfway until we leave LEFP territory." I clapped my hands together. "So let's move!"

"Don't be so certain you'll make it." Ohhhh, hoh-hoh. I was done with him. Completely and utterly, done. Especially after last night.

"I will put you in a ditch, you son of a–!"

"Xan?" Rowan cut my threat off.

"Nothing! Moving on!" My energy today was mammoth in size and I knew where it rooted. Kakó was beginning to leak more and more into me. His voice was getting louder and the pain had doubled, but my absorbance had tripled so I was now kept awake for everything. Using context clues, Kakó was extremely strong and powerful, which made me scared of him.

People were scared of him. And I was a part of him.

So they avoided me.

And for fifteen years, no one dared to tell me why.

"Hey, Xan, can I ask you a question?" Rowan asked me after a few minutes of walking.

"Sure," I responded, up front alongside Lijin.

"Last night...or this morning...or earlier...or yesterday? I-it doesn't really matter. Anyway, you said that the water moved with you, right? What's that about?"

"...? Oh. You're right, I did say that." I put my finger to my lips, thinking about the interaction. It was so blurry. I was so focused on the girl and Rowan. I couldn't exactly say what really happened. "I guess...that's just how it felt. That's my best explanation. I felt like I could move really easily and that instead of the density of the water fighting against me, it helped me move. Like it went with me." I shrugged. "But I was in a panic, so I don't know what–"

"Shh!" Lijin shot out his arm and stopped abruptly. I smacked into his hand.

"Ow!" I whined, rubbing my nose.

"Be quiet!" he whispered in return. He scanned the area. After one quick glance, I realized I couldn't see anything, so I closed my eyes and let my ears do all the work. The faint pumping of blood. The rustle of leaves. The spike in heart rate. Then the very small *"Now!"* And then the whistle of an object coming from...

I stuck out my hand to my right and, eyes still closed, pinched the knife between my fingers before it hit my face. Then I snapped my eyes back open, spun, and chucked the knife back to where it came from. It did not hit its target.

"Ooh. Foul ball," I said. The guys put their guards up, but I kept my posture calm. "I have no more to throw. Come on out." Indecision was passed back and forth in the bushes a little ways away. I cocked my head to the side when no one came out. "Okie dokie, then. Plan B, it is." I got on my knees and pawed through my bag until I found my pistol. *Here we go.* I set it up, letting its metal noise echo in the night. Then I aimed it at the bushes, estimated their height, went right above that, and pulled the trigger.

One of them squealed. She fell out into the open. She had long dark hair pulled up into a ponytail and her outfit was all too familiar: the uniform of an LEFP guard.

"Stand up, you stupid klutz!!" a male voice yelled. He sounded like he was somewhere around Lijin's age. He stepped out with his gun up. I read their name tags. T. Macendail was the guy and L. O'rell was the girl.

"You're early," I said, lowering my gun. "I hadn't expected to see any guards for at least another hour."

"We came by ourselves," O'rell said in return. Macendail kicked her.

"You guys are a long way from home. Let me help you get back," he told us.

"Nah, We can manage. Thanks, though. Bye!" I waved him off. Macendail snorted.

"Sorry. Not today."

"Oh, but I'd like today. You see, I've waited a *long* time for this and it's kind of a once in a lifetime opportunity. Can't turn it down. Maybe next time, though. Well, actually, I'd prefer it if I never had to see you guys again. Nothing against you guys, it's just–"

He fired at my forehead. I fell back and slammed against the ground. *Ow. That hurt.*

"Xan!!" Rowan, Jay, and Lijin screamed.

"You talk too much," Macendail said with an *"easy"* drip to his attitude.

My body moved faster than I was used to. Next thing I knew, I was standing behind him with my gun against his head and my hand on his shoulder.

"...?!"

"You boast too much," I whispered.

"*Kill him, child,*" Kakó ordered. I seriously considered it, which I hated myself for.

"H-how did you–?!"

"Dodge and act. It's easy. And deceivable," I told him. Macendail let out a nervous laugh. The expression "*keep her talking*" was written all over his face. Kakó chuckled through me and it frightened both the guard and myself. Then I noticed Macendail move.

I grabbed the knife that he was just about to stab into me. Then my hand started to move on its own and I did everything I possibly could to keep *my* body under *my* control. But despite my best efforts, I lost my grip.

"No, Kakó!!" I screamed, but he stabbed my hand into Macendail's side. The man fell to the ground and I followed. I pinned his body down, sitting on his chest. I wasn't too sure what unleashed this much control from him. It could've been my desire to leave, my anger that we were followed, or just the thrill of the situation. I couldn't tell. But no matter what it was, he was ready for bloodshed.

The knife was pulled out of him and stabbed into his shoulder. He went to grab his gun which had been knocked out of his hands and now laid beside us, but I held down his wrist. Then I yanked the knife out of his shoulder and placed it right above the center of his forehead. *No. N-no! This'll...this'll just make me more of a monster!!*

"Troy!!" O'rell shrieked at the same time the guys screamed my name.

"Xan, no!! Don't!" Lijin lunged to stop me, but I was too far away.

My hand was jammed down against my will.

Troy Macendail flinched, shutting his eyes. After a moment, he opened them back up again. No blood ran down his face. He was still alive. My left arm burst into agony and my head did the same as Kakó fought against my mark. But I stood my ground. I kept the knife above his face. It hurt and my hand shook. But I would not kill him.

"I am not a killer," I muttered. Who was I talking to? Honestly, I don't know. It could've been Sergeant Macendail, it could've been Kakó, and it also could've been myself. Or all three. But whoever it was, I wanted to let them know one thing: I would not be consumed by whatever was in me.

"I am not a killer," I said again, louder this time, directed at everyone around me. "Would if I could, mate, but I can't kill you. Not for your sake, I couldn't care less about what happens to you. But for the sake of me. He doesn't define me and I'm tired of people saying he does." I ripped the handcuffs out of his belt and, before he could do anything, I flung him out from under me, threw him against the tree, and cuffed him to its branches. O'rell was stunned. So were the boys and Lijin.

"You can follow us," I said, walking away, "but Troy is bleeding out and will die if you leave him here. So...it's your choice." As I expected, she decided to save Macendail instead of pursuing us, so we were off the hook for at least a little while. Rowan, Jay, and Lijin followed me away from the guards and we continued to head for the edge of the LEFP's property line.

It took them a little to gather themselves. Rowan finished first.

"Uhm...what the heck was that?!" he asked.

"I dunno," I responded kind of honestly.

"I thought you were shot!" he complained.

"So did the enemy. You let your guard down in triumph. It's a good thing to know."

"Xan," Lijin said.

"Yeah?" I replied, turning to him.

"You're relying on it too much."

"...? T-too much? He's probably the most unreliable thing out there! And I don't want to talk about it right now." I faced the opposite direction, trying to calm myself down. Rhekkun hopped off of Jay to run at my feet. I knew that she could most likely sense Kakó's presence in me, but it didn't seem to bother the small kitten.

Jay whistled at my huff.

"That'll be the last sound you make, you imbecile," I threatened.

"Oh, really?"

"Famous last words," Rowan said, bowing his head and clasping his hands together in prayer as if to mourn Jay's death. Lijin let out a childish laugh. Rowan erupted with him. Jaymon smirked. I smiled. My demon forgotten, we laughed over random things for the next hour. Then we sat down in a small patch of grass that was hit by the sun to eat. It was sandwiches–don't know what kind–that Lijin had snagged from the guard's eating quarters.

"What even is this?" Rowan asked.

"Don't know," Lijin told him. "If you're allergic, I'll have to bring flowers to your funeral, 'cause this is all I got." Something that I had learned over the past few hours was that Lijin might do anything for us. It was different from other people. Unreliable. So, how serious was he with that statement? Which side was I to believe?

"Better than prison food," Jay said. I placed the sandwich in front of me in my mouth and immediately agreed with him.

"Ha! You guys have it good. You should see what other prisons serve!" Lijin exclaimed.

"Hard pass," he replied.

"Thought so."

I'll wait it out, see which side I like better.

● ● ●

~8:49~

Crossing the mountains was easy and, miraculously, we didn't run into any guards. I know that they were right on our tails, but ever since the sun came up, we were able to move faster. Rowan was healing quickly, Jay didn't talk about his breakdown, and Kakó left me alone, so everything was good. Occasionally, though, a rock would try to enter my bloodstream through the heels of my bare feet. That never felt good. Perks of climbing a mountain without shoes. But if it meant freedom...it was only a small price to pay.

I unconsciously started humming.

"What song is that?" Lijin questioned after a minute or two. It took me a second to find what rhythm I was counting.

"*Looking at Me,* Sabrina Carpenter."

"So you've been using the music box?"

"Yes. It works pretty well."

"Glad you like it."

Rhekkun meowed so Jay stopped to pour some water in his hands for her to drink. She lapped it up gratefully. The cat had given up about twenty minutes ago and had been on his shoulders ever since.

"Hey, Lijin, what's the name of the lady who's taking us in?" Rowan asked as we began to continue climbing.

"Oh, uh...Meilynn." The name struck me as familiar and after a second, I was able to place it.

"Meilynn, like Meilynn Teraki? Like your mom, Meilynn?"

"What?!" Rowan exclaimed.

"So we're going to your mom's house?" Jay asked.

"Well...uh...sorta. Technically...in legal terms...yes, she's my mom."
He turned to me. "When–how did you figure out that that's who that was?"
Crap. I mean, I couldn't tell him that I had been sneaking around the LEFP.
Well, he knew that. Just not what I was specifically doing. I scrambled for an
answer. Then, thank God, something popped up in my vision and I was able
to change the subject.

Beyond where we were was a barbed wire fence and then a dirt road
that led out to the city. We had reached the top of the mountains. The end of
the LEFP's boundaries.

"Whoa!!"

"Wow."

"Awesome!!"

"Freedom!!" Rowan thrust up his hands and started to make his way
to the bottom.

"W-wait!" Lijin cried, laughing. "Hold up, Rowan!" I looked to Jay
who I was left standing with. The scene of his breakdown replayed itself in my
head. I brushed my braid behind my ear and stared out at the expanse in front
of us.

I said, "Don't know who Alice is, but I bet she'd be proud of how far
you've come." 'Alice.' It was the name he had muttered while he sobbed.

"...?"

I grabbed his wrist. "C'mon!"

"H-hey!! Slow down!"

I laughed.

When we made it to the fence, we stopped to study it. The top of it had those curly thingies that sliced you up into confetti when you touched them. Slicey sliceys usually hurt. Ain't no getting around that.

"No going over," I observed.

"Below ground's the same. No going under," Lijin told us.

Rowan glanced from side to side. "No going around."

"So we go through," Jay muttered.

"Guess so. But, uh...how?" I asked him.

"Simple." He set down Rhekkun and dug through his bag. Then he pulled out *pliers. Pliers!* Where could he possibly have gotten them? I didn't even want to know. "We cut our way through."

"W-wait," Rowan said reaching out to stop Jay from touching the fence. "Do we think it's electrified?" He glanced up at Lijin who stared at the wires for a few moments.

"Hmm. Good question, kid." He looked around at our surroundings. Then he spotted something off in the distance. His face lit up. "Here, wait here for a second." He dashed off towards whatever he had found.

Left with Rowan and Jay, we kinda just stared awkwardly at each other until Rowan pointed to the pliers and asked, "Where the hell you get those?" Jay shrugged.

"Y'know the place I raided to get the supplies for the traps I set?" he questioned. I shook my head.

"No," Rowan told him.

"Yeah, well, anyway, I found these." He held them up. "They should really have more guards in places like that. For being the best prison around and having six thousand sergeants, their security really ain't that great. Wire cutters would've been much better, but hey, I'll make do with what I got."

Lijin returned with a handful of some type of nuts. He ordered us to step back and then tossed them at the fence. Nothing happened. It was very boring to watch.

"What was that supposed to be?" I asked.

He smiled. "If the fence was electrified, then the nuts would've fried or burned." *Oh.* "So, since they didn't, we can cut through."

I'm surprised it worked, but a few minutes later, we were stepping through the metal. Finally, we were leaving! Leaving!

"One problem..." Lijin murmured. There was always a problem. "Since it isn't dark out anymore, we're kinda out in the–"

BWEEP-BWEEP!

"*Hey! Yeah, you! Back inside prisoners! And Teraki, you're under arrest for taking part in a potential breakout!*" a speaker yelled. Then a number of guards exited a group of cop cars and, with guns up, they began to run at us. Lijin ushered us through the fence.

"Potential?" he scoffed back. "I thought you knew me! I always finish what I've started." He threw out another smoke bomb. What was that going to do? We were outside. The wind would just blow the smoke away.

Then someone yelled, "*Crap!!* Get down!!" There was a loud explosion. It wasn't a smoke bomb. It was a grenade. Lijin had used a grenade on his comrades to save me and mine.

"Run!" he demanded. And we were off.

"Teraki!!" someone screamed through coughs.

"Naughty Teraki," Rowan scolded as we ran. "You need a timeout when we reach Mommy's house."

"Yeah, well, pipsqueak, sorry to disappoint you, but I don't get timeouts anymore," he told him. They both laughed.

"Bad Lijin. We don't blow up friends," I said, laughing with them.

"They weren't my friends. Does that still count?"

"...Guess not," Jay entered. I smacked his arm.

"Don't let him off the hook!"

"Well, *I'm sorry!*"

"Disapproval, Jaymon," Rowan said. We laughed. Then Lijin looked over his shoulder, back at the fence.

"They'll catch up soon."

"How far is Meilynn's house?" I asked him.

"Not far. Maybe five and a half miles. After the river"

"Then we cross through the river and then run for our lives for five miles. Literally."

So we picked up the pace.

sun bleached
to lose hope in salvation
and be ripped from my skin
to give up in a battle
 and let the other side win
to be betrayed by those
who were thought to be kin
my trust stretched to its limits
and my patience ran thin
the sun burns away my character
i'm left alone with my sins
when you've been through what i have,
you won't let anyone in

–PRISONER JOURNAL OF

SUBJECT 3029

Eighteenth   3029

Meilynn's house was large and painted a light blue with a white door and several windows. The garage was closed and there were chalk drawings scattered amongst the driveway and sidewalk. The plant life consisted of well treated flowers and a large oak tree in the center of the yard. On the tree was a wooden swing. A home for a family.

I looked down at my throbbing feet and dug my nails into my left hand. Did this woman know what she was in for? What if she rejected me? Could she do that? Would she?

"Xan," Lijin said. I looked up. Great, they were all turned around staring at me. Perfect. My face flushed. "She knows about you. And she doesn't care."

"...?"

He smiled. "She's dealt with a troublesome kid before. Mei's a pro at this kind of stuff. You guys are going to love her. Come on." He held out his hand to me in a fist. Rowan and Jay placed theirs up against his. I waited for Kakó to say something before I lifted my hand.

"*One free day,*" he said in Greek.

"What does that mean?" I whispered. They waited, knowing who I was talking to.

"*I'll give you one day to be on your own. Unless you need me.*"

"Seriously?" It was suspiciously kind of him, but if it meant he'd go away...I'd take it. I put my fist up against theirs before he could change his mind. "Okay. Let's go." Lijin nodded and walked us up to the door. He dug through his pockets then pulled out a silver key. He put it in the doorknob.

"You aren't even gonna knock?" Jay asked.

"Why would I knock on my own door?" That took all three of us by surprise.

"Whoa, whoa, whoa. You still live with your mom?" I questioned.

He muttered, "Yeah... Sort of." He then twisted the key, pulled it out, put it in his pocket, and then grabbed the knob.

"Sort of?"

"I've lived at the LEFP for the past four years." *True.* Lijin took a deep breath in, let it out, then turned the knob and pushed the door open.

The interior was beautiful. A sea glass green room was to our right with white carpet, two white couches with pillows, a ledge at the large window, a 52 inch TV, and a rectangular glass table. That was the first thing I noticed. To our left was a dark blue office with plants, a computer, bookshelves, lots of paper, and a black office chair. Lijin shut the door and it made me jump.

"I'm home," he called.

"Lijin?!" A tall, young-looking adult woman with long dark brown hair and beautiful caramel skin popped around the corner in front of us. She ran up to us, stopping a few feet away. I still backed up, bumping into Rowan.

"Hi," she said to us. Then she turned to Lijin. "So this is them?"

"Yep," Lijin replied. "Jaymon, Rowan, and Xandralin." He pointed to each of us in turn. Jay's cat meowed, angry that she'd gone unnoticed. "Oh, and this is Rhekkun. Guys, this is Mei." Rowan waved, Jay nodded, and I stared.

"I have rooms prepared for all of you, if that's okay," Mei told us.

"You do?" Rowan asked.

"I do." Just then a little girl bounded down the stairs. She had dark skin like Meilynn and she had dark curly pigtails that bounced as she ran.

"*Li Li!!*" she yelled. She jumped up into Lijin's arms and he struggled to not drop her. Then he smiled, laughing.

"Hey, Litz! Goodness, you're so big! Where's Sam?" I assumed Litz was his sister. I assumed the same for Sam.

"Right here." On the stairs was a girl a little younger than me with red hair that was tied back in a long braid. She cocked her head to the side when we made eye contact. I shrank back. "Who're they?"

"Sam, they're going to stay with us for a little while," Mei explained.

"Oh. Okay. Sup, Lijin. Didn't think you were coming."

"Heyyy. I made a last minute decision." He set down Litz and Sam walked over to us. Mei clapped her hands together.

"Okay, so rooms. I have two spare bedrooms. I figured boys and girl?" I glanced at Jay and Rowan. Great. Alone again. I didn't want to be alone. "*Or*...Sam has offered for you to stay with her if you'd like, Xan." Her use of my nickname caught me off-guard. She seemed to sense my surprise. "Oh, uh, sorry! Lijin just talks about you with the use of that name. Habit. Hehe. I can call you Xandralin if you'd prefer it."

This woman was casually talking to me. Using my name. Looking me in the eye. Smiling. I couldn't trust it. I decided to keep my guard up.

"Uh, no. Xan's okay. And...I guess..." I took a second to decide. I wasn't sure that I wanted to be with Lijin's sister, but I didn't want to force Jay and Rowan to be together. Or be by myself. "...I can try...being...with Sam. If that's alright," I replied. Sam smiled.

"Okay! You guys can settle in! Lijin, take the boys. Samrinn–"

"Got it. C'mon!" She ran for the stairs. Then up them. I stood at the bottom as Mei passed me. Something slid into my right hand. I looked over in surprise. It was Rowan's fingers.

"You gonna be alright?" he asked. I wanted to be honest with him. But what would he think about my distrust in the only opening people I'd met? Judgment? Disgust? I couldn't take either. So I shook his hand.

"Yeah, I'll be fine," I replied. Jay walked up and tapped our hands.

"We're free, guys. We got out," he said.

"Yeah. He's right," Rowan responded. The boys smiled. I forced my face muscles to mimic their actions. Sam poked her head back down the stairs.

"You coming?" she asked. After a moment, I responded with a stiff nod. I let go of the hands held in mine and climbed the staircase. Two days ago I was talking to my parents through phones, behind glass, with guards watching my every move. Now, I was in someone else's house, without my number being my name, on the other side of the bars. I guess, I was happy with the change, with the freedom, but I still wanted to know why Lijin had so suddenly decided to break us out. "I'll tell you later," he had told me. How much later did it have to be?

We went up the stairs, taking a 90 degree turn to the right halfway and then turning left down the hallway at the top. Sam led me into the first room on the right. I found myself in a coral room with a white desk, short carpet, a small window, wooden bunk bed, several picture frames, a dresser, and a flag. Sam had me set my stuff down on the top bunk. She spun around on the floor.

"Well, this is my room! You're welcome to touch basically anything. It's all mine, so you're good as long as nothing's lost or broken."

My attention was drawn to the flag. *All hers, huh?* I pointed to it. "Is that yours?" She flushed beet red. "What country is that?" I didn't recognize the colors.

"What? C-country? Well, uh, n-no. It's, I just–my friend. It, uh, it means..." she stuttered. "Y-you know what? It doesn't matter." I glanced back and forth between her and the flag.

"I think it's cool. Pretty colors," I said.

"Oh. Y-you do?"

"Yeah." She looked away from me.

"The, uh, the flag represents demisexuality. I-it's not really a big deal. Just something small that Mom let me get..." Her voice slowly faded away and her entire face boiled red. I still wasn't sure what...whatever she called it...was.

"*She's gay, idiot,*" Kakó muttered. *Ohhhh.*

My thing with the LGBTQ+ community was that I had never actually met someone that was a part of it, so there was nothing for me to judge. Actually, if anything, I found them interesting. The religion that my parents practiced and I was forced into, thought that their way of loving was wrong. Though I saw it like this: these people didn't fit the "normal" standard and still had the guts to tell people about it. They were unique so some people hated them. It was just like how I was treated. But I couldn't even bear the *thought* of telling people about my mark. Let alone actually do it. And on top of that, Sam had said that Mei had gotten her the flag.

So her mom supported her.

Sam's flag had a black triangle on the left, a purple stripe across the middle, white on the top half, and gray on the bottom half. Demi, I guess.

Still blushing, she tried to move the subject away from the flag.

"So, uh, your name's Xan, right?"

"Yeah." I slowly sat down on the corner of the bottom bunk which was turned 90° to form a sort of cross shape with the upper half. She plopped down in front of me.

"And Mom says you came from where my brother works. Prison. I-is that...really true?" she asked.

"...?" I righted myself, not quite sure how to respond, but not wanting her to notice. "It...it is."

"Can I hear about it?" *What? She...wants to hear about it?*

"*Do* you...want to hear about it?"

"Well, I mean, yeah. I wouldn't have asked if I didn't actually want to know," she said with a smile. So I started to tell her about it. I started talking.

Sam wasn't that bad. I kind of liked her. I was scared to, but as we talked, I let my body loosen up a bit. I calmed down. And the way she acted reminded me of Lexi. Honest, smart, wholehearted. And, honestly, that hurt. Lexi had been fine with being my friend. One of the very few. And I had left her. I decided to try to make things right with Sam, be kind, get her to like me as much as I could. Save *this* Lexi. It was all I could do.

● ● ●

We were sat down in white chairs at a long wooden table. Plates of well made home cooked food were set in front of us. Litz clasped her little hands together and mumbled a small prayer that only half made sense. Then she shouted, "Amen!!" and dug into her meal. Sam rolled her eyes and ate slowly.

Rowan and Jay both drooled, but held themselves back. I just stared at my lap. Was it okay for us–prisoners–to enjoy such a meal? I felt out of place here. Too clean. Too nice. Too much freedom. There had to be a trick here, right?

Beside me, Lijin leaned over to whisper in my ear, "You can eat it. You don't have to act like a prisoner. You aren't one anymore. Do what you want. No guards are monitoring you."

"Besides you," is all I responded with, my tone dripping acid.

"Hey, I broke you out. You can trust me. Right?"

"I haven't decided." It was an honest reply. It was also something I had meant to keep to myself. I flushed at my lack of control over what I say. I expected Lijin to be hurt or taken aback. But he just smiled.

"That's okay." He raised his voice back to its normal volume as he pulled away from me. "Rowan, Jay, go ahead. You can have it." They immediately responded with nods and started to eat their lunch. I waited. It was abnormal. The kindness we were being shown. Was I the only one who saw it?

"No tricks," Lijin muttered. I hesitantly reached for my plate.

Until my head and arm exploded with pain. I screamed and grabbed my face. Everyone jumped. My blood was splattered across the table. I could feel my mark spread, my skin burn, and my flesh tear. I stood up and stumbled away from the table.

"Xan, don't stand up!!" Lijin yelled, his chair screeching as he jackknifed to his feet. But I didn't listen to him, I didn't care. I could stand if I wanted to, it didn't matter. Right now, I was just furious.

"You said you'd leave me alone!!" I screeched.

"*I did!!*" Kakó yelled back.

"Then what is going on?!"

Litz curled into a ball in terror. Sam lost color, frightened. Mei stood with Jay and Rowan. When I got no response from Kakó and my pain increased, I lost it.

"Kakó, answer me!!" I yelled. I was then pushed to my knees and my vision was clouded with four images.

A girl with bright yellow eyes, curled up in the tail of a horrifyingly large wolf. A boy with glowing green eyes, wrapped in a giant serpent. A boy with fluorescent red and orange eyes, consumed by a huge fox. And a boy with deep black eyes, shadowed by a terrifyingly big crow.

Then another image showed up.

A girl with shining white eyes, surrounded by a humongous dragon.

I couldn't make out who the people were. I could just see their eyes and the horrifying creatures.

"Who...are...they?"

"Xan!" Rowan called. He sounded distant. Then he faded farther away. And then he was gone. Only darkness remained.

As of now, I have one creation that suits my needs. Her name is Ilo_773. She is a combination of fish, human,, panther, and a secret something that no one but me needs to know about. She is trained to find whoever I command.

Goodbye dear.

Ilo is out for you.

G. Qinglee

–EXPERIMENT JOURNAL OF
SERGEANT 0001

nineteenth

He waited patiently. He knew she'd come. She'd be let in this time. He swished his long scaly tail back and forth in the darkness. The ground was wet, about a foot of water covering everything with little clouds of fog that lingered here and there.

She screamed for an answer. It echoed.

Kakó stayed silent. His pointed teeth glowed as his lips curled up overtop of them. A few short images passed through the girl's head. Then she lost consciousness.

"Soon..." he crowed to himself.

After a moment, he could hear something move in the water. It staggered and moved slowly, cautiously. He slithered across the glassy liquid until he found her.

She was tall, lengthy. She had short black hair that was braided on the left side. The black hair looked just like the woman's. Her violet eyes matched the man's. When she noticed him, she froze. Her face filled with terror and she stepped back. He ate the reaction up, satisfied.

"W...what the f–rick?!"

He smirked. "Welcome, child."

"But you're...you can't be...!" she cried.

"Ha ha. But that is where you are wrong, kiddo. Of course I can," he replied. "In fact, I am."

"...K...Kakó?" He smiled as he drew himself higher.

He was around fifty times taller than her. Give or take. His scales were a marble of three different colors: blue for water, purple for night, and magenta for blood. His eyes were slightly bloodshot with slim, catlike pupils and white, foggy irises. He had a pink scar running along his left back thigh. His teeth were long, sharp, yellowed, and dripping saliva.

The perfect image for the 2nd Great Terror.

Kakó adored the pulsing fear in the girl. As a Terror, no one would ever even *dare* look down upon him. And he absolutely loved it.

"...You're...what's...inside...?" She couldn't even finish her sentence as she gawked. Then she shook her head, trying to right herself. "...W-where am I?"

He ignored her question. "So, tell me again your name."

"...X-Xandralin. Xandralin Raq."

"...?" Though he'd expected the name, it still managed to catch him by surprise. Kakó hadn't heard *that* name in fifteen years. She was her spitting image. Young, frightened, tough, kind, alone.

"Raq, you say?" He circled around her, his claws skimming the water as she watched. "Haven't heard that name in a while."

"What does that mean?" She spun slowly, trying to keep eye contact.

"Well, RJ, you aren't the first to come in here."

"What'd you call me? Wait, then who was first? And I still don't know where '*here*' is." Her questions piled with every word he spoke.

"I called you 'RJ', Raq Junior. The first was dear Alicia." He left out question three. He slowly rotated his body as he circled her until he floated around with his stomach in the air.

"...A-Alicia?" He knew the name sparked a memory in her. One that wouldn't make sense. But he did not elaborate. He loved leaving missing pieces to a puzzle. That's what made it fun. "Isn't that the name of one of–"

"There are only so many names in the world. But it's a small world," he replied, leaving all options open. RJ looked down in confusion. Kakó stopped and spun to an upright position.

"So how is Alicia related to me? Or, like, how come you're...in...me and not her?" she asked.

"Because she is dead and you are not," he responded flatly.

"But...I mean, was she your vessel?"

"Yes."

"I-I thought you died if your vessel..."

"Not under some circumstances."

"Like what?"

His smile widened. She clenched her jaw, feeling uneasy. Damn, was this gonna confuse the hell outta her.

He explained, "If the vessel dies giving birth, the Terror is passed to the surviving child."

"...?!" The color drained from her face when she processed it. She stepped away from him. "B-but my mom...is still..."

"She is?" Kakó waited.

"Y-yes! Abagail–!"

"Since when was she your mother, dear child?" he questioned.

"S-since forever! A-Abagail is my birth mother!" RJ defended.

"Interesting." He looked up at the dark abyss above them. "Because I seem to know otherwise."

"She looks just like me! We have the same last name! She raised me!" She dug her nails into her left hand. He ignored it.

"Ever heard of a relative? And "raised" is putting quite a spin on it, don't you think?" She wouldn't accept it. She just continued to deny it, raising her voice.

"I don't have any relatives!! Just my mom and dad!!" she yelled. He slithered through the air around her.

"Aunt and uncle," he corrected.

"What?! Kakó, quit it! H-how could–?"

"Your mother loved you. Your aunt does not."

"B-but, if Abagail's not my mom, then..."

"You've been lied to your entire life about yet another crucial asset of your background?" he offered. She dropped her hands. Her voice was launched from an agonizing scream to a tumbling whisper.

"...Yeah. Th-the only people I thought loved me at some point... because I was their child...aren't even my parents..."

"Do not take it too harshly, RJ. The truth hurts."

Xan fell to her knees without a word. Something slid down her cheek and created ripples in the water that steamed with mist for a scarce moment.

"So I didn't even get to meet my mom..." she muttered.

"Her body couldn't take keeping me in and letting you out. It killed her." Kakó concealed all emotion. He just flat out told her that her mother had died bringing her into the world. He could see that she blamed it on herself immediately.

"What about my dad?"

"Died protecting you." That hit her hard.

"So...both my parents...died...because of me...?"

"That's one way to put it," he responded.

"*...Knhg...ungh...*" The girl began to sob. With her feelings intensified, she wouldn't be able to contain any of her overwhelming grief. Kakó didn't want to push her in fear that she might eventually try to do something to harm herself because it would bring about great consequences to him. So he let her tears run. After a bit, RJ curled up into a ball, hugging her knees.

"...Where am I?" she murmured between sobs. "I wanna go back..."

"You're in the chamber in which I am held within your body," he told her.

"Why?" He couldn't tell what she was asking about. The parents, the place, where he was held? Could've been anything. He waved his front talon.

"You're going to have to be more specific than that."

"Why am I confined to you?!" she screamed in an outburst. "I never asked for you!! I never signed up for this!!"

"There was no sign-up, Xandralin. It's your calling," Kakó informed.

"Calling?! To be a demon house for the rest of my life, that's my *calling?!*" She stood up and the air shook.

"Look, you think I *enjoy* being cooped up in a little girl for all of eternity?!" Kakó yelled back, his own rage bubbling. RJ instinctively stepped back in fear, but then stepped forward with twice as much emotion.

"*You* don't get the looks, the rumors, the fights, the loneliness!!"

"Yeah, but your mother did."

That stopped her.

"And I watch through your guys' eyes. I still have to deal with it, I still see and hear it." He watched all the fight drain out of the girl. She was no longer angry; she was just sad. Just upset.

"Yeah, but...you're...the one who's causing it all..." Tears streamed in lazy rivers down her red cheeks.

"I didn't ask to be put in you, child. It just happened. I had no say in the situation, I could not change the outcome. I am the Dragon Of The Mist. And I always will be. It is my calling," he told her.

She put her hand up in a 'stop' gesture. "Please, just stop talking about callings."

"What am I supposed to call it, then? My destiny? My job? A destiny you can change, a job you choose." He swiveled his tail, trying to calm down. "Look. Maybe...we can just...make this work."

"I'm not killing anyone!!" she yelled automatically.

"Fine, fine, fine. Just–"

"I won't kill my family! Stop offering!"

"A family that doesn't want you, RJ! They see you as a freak!"

"Well, so does everyone else!!"

"Alicia–"

"You let Alicia die!!"

"I couldn't save her. There was nothing I could do." Kakó gritted his sharp teeth at the young girl's stubbornness. Now *that* was just like the boy. She took after all three of them.

"You take over me all the time! Couldn't you have just–?!"

"Your seal is weaker! I couldn't do those things with her!" he argued.

"What about this? Could she do this?" She meant could she come to talk face to face with him. That brought up puddles of memories of him sitting with the girl in the water, chatting for hours. Now those moments he missed.

"The girl came more often than you'd think sane."

"...?" She hadn't expected that. The dragon pulled himself closer to the stunned girl.

"In fact, she came to see me just before she died. She told me to be kind to you."

RJ scoffed, still slightly crying. "You haven't been very good at that."

"I woke you up to the world," he said. "How much kinder do you want me to be? I am not sure what you're truly wanting from me, child." She stared him dead in the eye, something most people couldn't do.

"If that's your definition of 'kind', then just stop. I'm already used to living without kindness. Why would I want it now? And from *you*, of all people?"

"You clearly don't trust me," Kakó observed, starting to smile.

"Why would I?" she growled.

"Because I am the only person you *can* trust right now," he replied.

"And you're more trustworthy than anyone else?"

"If you die, I die. So you can trust that I'll keep you alive." She considered it and then grumbled and turned away. Kakó grinned in triumph. Then something hit the girl.

"Wait, if she came all the time, then–"

"Yes. I can send you back," he told her with a nod.

"Please, do!"

"Fine." She beamed and fresh tears streamed down her face. "Oh, and, RJ?"

"...Yeah?"

"Callings aren't painless." She locked her jaw, shifting her weight. "But that doesn't necessarily mean they have to be painful."

"...? What does–?" Before she could finish, Kakó sent her consciousness back to her world. Her body changed into mist and floated up with the rest of the fog.

Alicia. She'd had short black hair, a freckled face, bright blue eyes, rosy cheeks, and a bright smile. The girl had been broken. Beaten down by verbal assumptions about her and Kakó. She'd grown up without parents, nobody to cry to. The first time she'd met the dragon, she'd been a bit scared, instinctively, but she'd quickly realized that she now had someone to talk to and that took over her fear. He'd thought she'd be frightened, but she broke down in tears for the wrong reason.

"*Why aren't you scared?*" Kakó had demanded.

"*I have someone who'll talk to me. Someone who knows me,*" she'd responded with. She was the first to look at him and not his title. And after a while, Kakó realized that Alicia accepted him more than the 5 Great Terrors did.

That's why it had burned so much when she died.

"*Teach her about life. Let her know that she's not alone in this hell that we live in. And, Kakó, let Xan know that I love her.*" It was her last request. He nodded that day.

"*Of course. Anything. She's part you, after all.*"

She smiled. Then she stroked his long snout.

"*Take care of them.*"

"*Will do.*"

Then she'd left for the afterlife. Leaving him all alone. He'd been more devastated than he had ever felt in his entire life.

Kakó chuckled, pulling out of the memory.

"You aren't going easy on me, are you, kiddo?" There was no response because he hadn't sent it to her. "These Raqs. All four of you. So much trouble." He laughed to himself. Then settled down in the water. "Oh well, she'll come around. After all, the boy did. *Tah.* For a little while, anyway."

In all my life I've had three friends. Daniel, Jay, and Xan. One thing I've noticed is that I seem to attract people who aren't completely whole anymore. I mean:

Jay's scarred,

Xan's broken,

and Daniel...committed suicide.

What is it that brings shattered people to me? I mean, not like I'm capable of fixing them. I figured that out a long time ago.

–PRISONER JOURNAL OF

SUBJECT 5742

twentieth 1863

She shot up, tears streaming down her face.

"Wait–!" She reached out her hand.

"Xan, n-no one's leaving," I said. I was sitting at her side on the floor in the dining room. Rowan was across from me while Lijin and Mei were on their knees at her feet. Litz was upstairs in her room and Sam was watching from the doorway that led into the kitchen to our left.

She let her hand fall. "Y-yeah, I know."

"Xan, who were you talking to?" Lijin asked. I quickly noticed that she wouldn't look at him. What was that about?

"No one." She stood up and Rowan and I stood with her. She touched her face. Then wiped her eyes.

"You started crying a few minutes ago," Rowan whispered. "What happened?" She looked around, but never actually made eye contact with any of us.

"I'll tell you later." Now, that had 'faulty promise' written all over it.

"But–"

"Guys, give me a bit, okay?" Rhekkun stood on her hind legs to paw at her. I called her over, but she ignored me. Xan picked her up, tenderly.

Something was different in her. She looked numb. Like something incomprehensible had just happened. But she'd been out cold. Had Mist talked to her? Was it able to talk to her if she passed out? What did it tell her?

Xan stared at my cat in her hands. "It has to be a coincidence, right?" she muttered to herself.

"What has to be a coincidence?" Rowan asked.

"Nothing."

"Lies," I said. She grinned a forced smile. Then her teeth parted for her to say something until she closed them. Hard. I could hear them creak against each other as she pressed her jaw together with so much force, it had to've hurt. Though, maybe that was what she wanted. Then her eyes kind of darted around like she was too afraid to look at one spot for too long. She seemed to be searching for what to respond with. Then Lijin stepped in.

"Xan, why don't you take Rhekkun and Sam and go lie down," he offered. She nodded, clearly relieved. She turned and I reached out my hand to stop her, but she dashed away.

"It did something to her," Lijin observed.

"Clearly."

"We're losing time."

"Well, then, let's get on with it," Mei said. "Jaymon?"

"Yeah?" I responded.

"Come with me." That took me by surprise.

"What? Where? Why me?" She didn't answer any of my questions.

"First, we have to do something about your subject number." I reached up and touched my neck with my fingertips. I had completely forgotten that it was there. Another thing that pointed us out as prisoners.

"What do you have in mind?"

Next thing I knew, I was sitting on her bed as she rummaged through her bathroom. Lijin and Rowan were together in Lijin's room so I was alone until Litz ran in. I didn't notice her–I was staring out the window–until I turned to find her on the bed, up against me, with her face closer than I let my toothbrush get.

"*Aghk!!*" I threw my body away from the child, creeped out. "What are you doing?!" I asked her. Mei peeked around the corner at us.

"Litz, leave Jay alone, sweetie."

"Where's your shoes?" she questioned, pointing to my bare feet and ignoring her mom.

"I, uh, don't have any..."

"Neither does Rowan or San."

"Sam?"

"Xan," Mei corrected from the other room. "She pronounces her '*Z*'s as '*S*'s." Something slammed shut and then something else was opened and gutted as she searched for whatever she was looking for.

"Oh."

"Found it!" She came out of the bathroom with tan colored bandages and scissors (because most people keep scissors in their bathroom?). She sat down beside me and told me to stay still. Then she wrapped them around my neck, over my tattoo. It was weird. This woman had escapees in her house and she was just covering up their subject numbers. Like, how did she find that normal? How was she okay with this? It was such a large crime and she was committing it so smoothly. I watched her as she spun the bandages around my throat.

"You see, I don't care that you're prisoners," she said suddenly, as if reading my thoughts. "I've always had a knack for seeing past what I'm given. You guys are just children. Powerless against what the world has in store for you. I feel that that isn't a reason enough to lock someone up." She finished, cut the bandages, and got up to put the rest of them back. She had me stand.

"Litz, go annoy Li Li, darling." The little girl bubbled with laughter saying, "Okay!" and then she ran off. Mei giggled before she turned her attention back to me. "Jay, would you want shoes? I don't have any for you right now, but I could get you some."

To accept such an offer felt wrong.

"No, I-I'm okay."

She cocked her head, not truly wanting to take my word. Then she smiled. "If you say so. Alright. Let's head out. We're gonna walk so that my license plate can't be recognized." She still didn't say where we were headed as we climbed back down the stairs.

"You still haven't told me where we're going," I said.

"We'll be back!" Mei called up the stairs before we left the house. Then she finally turned to me and said, "We're going to Xan's house." I was not expecting that.

"Xan's house? She doesn't live there. What do you need?"

"Her parents live there and they have information about the ritual that we don't." We started down the sidewalk.

"So you know where they live?"

"Lijin told me."

"Well, why does *he* know where they live?" I asked.

"He's her guard. They tell guards more than you'd think." She was so calm about it. But I still had so many questions.

"So why do you need me?"

"Because you're a good liar." God, she was quick and good.

"What? I don't lie!" That was a lie.

"Jaymon, I've raised four kids. I know a liar when I see one." That rotated the topic for most of the rest of the walk.

"Four? Lijin, Litz, and Sam makes three," I pointed out. The woman beside me watched where we were going while I just watched her, waiting for a response.

"Yes, well, I adopted all of them. At one point in time, I had my own child. Lijin is the only one who remembers him. He died the year Sam was born, three years before she was adopted," Mei told me with a pained smile on her face.

"...W-what was his name? And how did he die?"

"Ethaniel. And he died of COVID." I had never heard of COVID. Well, actually, I think that some of the older subjects talked about it from time to time, but I wasn't sure exactly what it was.

"What's COVID?" I asked.

"COVID or COVID-19 is short for Coronavirus. It hit the world in 2020. It only stayed in Bludriss for about a year. Ethan was born sick so he caught it very easily and it made him very ill. He was very good at detangling lies. That's why he and Lijin got along so well. The boy was devastated when we lost Ethan to that virus right before they found a cure."

No wonder I didn't remember it. I was only four.

"So Lijin lied a lot?"

"Oh, yes. You guys might not notice now, but he was very broken as a child. I found Lijin in his darkest moment. He was criticized for who he was, so he decided to lie about everything. He locked up all of his emotions until the day Ethan died and years of loneliness poured out of the kid." She didn't elaborate. And I didn't ask for more.

The rest of the walk was just silence.

We reached a dark house with a small porch. Mei led me up the stairs and over to the door. She knocked on it instead of ringing the doorbell.

"Coming, coming!!" The voice was female and sounded annoyed. The woman who opened the door had a long black braid that was draped loosely over her right shoulder and green eyes that were framed by rectangular glasses. She was wearing shorts, a teal shirt that said something about taking shifts talking to people and it wasn't our turn, and a long purple sweater. In her hand was a burning cigarette.

"Oh," she said with disgust. "It's you, Meilynn." I realized with a start that this was the first time I'd ever seen Xan's mom. She shared some similarities appearance wise with her, but she was still much different than I'd expected her to be. She was also much meaner.

"Hello, Abagail," Mei said with a friendly tone.

"Another?" she asked instead of returning the greeting. She was staring at me. I took a step back.

"Uh, yeah. This is Jay." I kept my hands in my pockets.

"Okay, well, I'm actually working online at the moment, so–" Mrs. Raq tried to shut the door but Mei stopped the door from closing with her foot.

"We won't take up too much of your time," she said. There was a click behind her back. I couldn't tell what it was.

"My class has started a historical unit on the 5 Great Terrors. I want to know how to perform the ritual to reseal them back inside of their vessels. I won't use your name or anything, but I will find a way to give you credit," I lied fluently. I thought she'd try to deny me, but after a moment, she bought the story and fed into it.

"So you came to me for information to help you with your homework because you believe that I want to provide you with that?" She stuck the cigarette in her mouth.

"I told him that you've been given a gift. You have all the knowledge, but you aren't a monster," Mei told her. It didn't sit right with me how she had explained it. Even if it was just an act to try to get her to agree.

Abagail puffed out smoke. "...Fine." She had us sit down in chairs on the porch. Mrs. Raq adjusted herself and then drew in a deep breath, rolling her eyes and talking fast without enthusiasm.

"First, you have to have five candles. Purple, yellow, orange, green, and black. You light four of them and have one person hold each, forming a square. You have to draw the seal pattern on the floor for that specific Terror vessel. You then draw a cross on their forehead and have them sit in the middle. They hold the remaining candle and it should eventually light on its own.

"Then, all four candle holders will chant, '*Exorístike apó ton Parádeiso kai tin Kólasi ston kósmo mas. Enklovisménos sti Gi mésa se aftí tin psyche'* which roughly translates to 'Banished from Heaven and hell to our world. Caged on Earth inside this soul' in English from Greek.

"The vessel will be resealed and the Terror will be trapped inside once again." She waved her hand around matter-of-factly while she put the cigarette back up to her lips. Something clicked underneath the table by Mei again. I glanced at her, but didn't mention anything about the sound. "So, am I, like, getting paid for this or...?"

"Oh, yes." Mei dug through her back pocket and then reached out and handed her about fifty bucks. Mrs. Raq swiped the money and counted it greedily before she stuffed it in the pocket of her sweater. My God, woman, why would you pay this psychopath?

"That's all we needed. Thank you." She stood up and waved for me to follow after she bowed. I bowed as well.

"Thanks," I muttered. As we walked, I tried going over the Greek words, but I couldn't remember them all. "Okay, so, like, did you even catch any of that? And what was the–" Meilynn held up a small box. There were four buttons on it: Play/Pause, Rewind, Forward, and Record. She had recorded what Abagail had said during the interview. Smart. "Oh."

"Did you really think I was going to make you memorize all of that? I may be in my 40s, but I'm not stupid, dear. And I used the tape recorder because if something happens to my phone, then we would lose it. And this can't be tracked. I've thought this through." I let myself smile for a second. I kinda liked her. "I'll get the candles now. I'll need to drive for that one, though, so I'll get my keys from inside the house. You also can't come with me. But you'll be okay. Then we can do the ritual tomorrow morning. Give Xan a night to calm down. How's that sound?"

Sounded fine to me.

As long as tomorrow wasn't too long of a wait. I didn't want to lose her. I wanted to save her. Stop her attacks, her outbursts. Get Mist to leave her alone. I wanted the old Xan back. I was scared of her now. She was unleashed and with everything swirling inside her head, she became confused and dangerous. I'd seen that before and I didn't want her to have to go through it.

I lost my sister because I'd lost *myself* for a *second*.

And Xan was a thousand times more dangerous than me.

Just think of what could happen.

"Jaymon?"

"Oh, uh, yeah. Sounds good."

She stopped walking. "She's going to be fine."

"You guys all keep saying that, but do you really believe it?" I questioned, stopping beside her.

"I do."

"Lijin never sounds sure. He always just sounds desperate. It's pathetic! He's placing hope in us that he doesn't even believe is possible himself! I mean, who does that?"

"Lijin lost hope in the world a long time ago. But he still believes that there is a chance when it comes to her." I found myself angry at that response.

"You keep talking about this depressed, distanced, alone person! Lijin seems fine! He doesn't act like that!"

"He's numb to it, Jaymon. He's watched his parents die three times. He's lost two siblings. His world has shattered over and over again."

"...?" I looked down, my face starting to burn. I didn't know that.

"We all have our own story. And sometimes we subconsciously choose someone to not read thoroughly. I can tell that as a kid, you were never read as much as you should've been. It's the same with Rowan, Xan, and Lijin. You have to give everyone a chance. Don't judge a book by its cover," she lectured.

"That's madly overused," I muttered. Mei smiled. She knew.

"C'mon. Let's go." We resumed walking until we made it to the house. I ran upstairs to find everyone else while Mei tossed down the tape recorder on the coffee table and searched for her keys to get ready to go and buy the candles.

Lijin and Rowan were both still in Lijin's room. Rowan was laying on the ground like a dead body and Lijin was on his bed, scrolling through his phone.

"What's going on?" I asked as I stepped over Rowan. He grabbed my ankle as I went by.

"Save me!!"

"Shh!! You're supposed to be dead," Lijin scolded.

"Oh yeah."

Dude, I was so freaking confused. Then a little girl sprang out of the closet and attacked me with a styrofoam sword.

"Got you! I got you, Jay!" Litz cried.

"You left and Sam locked her door, so guess who got to play with the 5-year-old?" Lijin told me.

"Heh." Litz continued beating my legs. "Sorry, I guess."

"Ah! He's too stwong!" Litz cried with dramatic hand motions. "How do we defeat 'im?" Then something went wrong in my head. I don't know what triggered it, but I was suddenly very annoyed.

"You can't," I told her.

"Why not? I got Li Li."

"Because it's just a game," I snapped unintentionally,

"Hey, whoa. Don't be mean to the kid," Rowan said.

"You need to get serious! You act like everything's fine!" I spiked. He sat up. Lijin shut off his phone.

"I'm just playing with her," Rowan grumbled.

"Well, quit. We have more important things to do." Litz stayed silent.

"Jay, there's nothing *to* do right now."

"Xan had another attack, woke up yelling and crying, won't even *look* at Lijin, and you guys are playing with a 4-year-old like nothing's wrong!" There was a tug on my shirt. "What?!"

"I'm five," Litz informed.

"Same thing!!"

"No." She held out four of her little fingers. "Four is dis many. Five is *dis* many." Her thumb popped up. I had to grind my teeth together to keep from either screaming at her or myself.

"Are you alright?" Lijin asked me. Honestly, I didn't know. Nothing had happened while I was out to make me act like this. Was it just all that had happened over the last few days?

I closed my eyes and combed my hair back. "I-I-I'm fine. Just...tired." I made sure my bangs had fallen back in front of my left eye before I opened it. Rowan stood and sat down on the bed at the same time I did. I held my head in my hands and sighed. Litz tapped on my knee.

"Sorry..."

It took me a second to respond. "I-it's fine."

"I was just–"

"Just give me a second, Ali–" I stopped myself and smacked my hand to my lips. My fingers were trembling. I hadn't called anyone that name in a long time.

"Jay, my name's Lits."

"I-I know," I said, stumbling to the door.

Lijin stood up. "Jay–"

"I-I have to go." I fell out the door, hitting the wall as I staggered away. Litz overlapped with Alice, Alice overlapped with Litz. I hit my head. They looked nothing alike. Sure, they acted a bit similar, but enough to make me mix up their names?

"What is wrong with you?!" I muttered to myself.

Good question. Nobody could figure it out.

When I was 15 I watched my older brother die. That just about killed me because as a kid, I went through literal hell. My parents were murdered in front of me. Then my adoptive mom died and my adoptive dad was killed. Then I had all that was left stolen from me. And when I finally opened up, Ethan died. I was so devastated. And guess what? Once I finally recovered, my current father died.

The kid that went through all of that is dead. I mean, how much trauma can a teen endure? It was easier to change and move away than it was to suffer and try to move on.

–GUARD JOURNAL OF

SERGEANT 7560

twenty-first 7560

Litz ran off to Mei and I was left alone with Rowan.

"Everyone's falling apart," he muttered. I couldn't blame him. Xan was getting worse by the minute, not to mention her attacks, and it was merging with her faster than what fit my likings. And of course Jaymon was losing his cool and breaking down. And I didn't know anything about him, so there was nothing for me to try and fix.

"They'll be fine." I wanted to put faith in those words, but the promise would not fill. Rowan stood up and walked to the front of the room. He touched the doorframe then turned back to face me.

"I don't take kindly to empty promises. So they better be okay. Your life might depend on it." I swallowed and he shut the door. It only took a few minutes before Meilynn showed up. She closed the door softly behind her and just stood there. I didn't care. I stared at the ground until she said something.

"What are you sulking for?" Mei asked.

"Xan is...Xan, Jay is distanced and having mental breakdowns, and Rowan now hates me," I groaned.

"He doesn't hate you," she said, crossing her arms. I rolled my eyes.

"Oh, really? You think so? He just threatened me, Mei."

"Over...?"

"Xan and Jay getting better," I muttered.

"Exactly." I looked up. She was leaning against the wall with her arms still folded across her chest. Her blue eyes watched my face carefully.

"What?" I questioned, not understanding.

Mei started to walk over to my bed. "He's protective over his friends." I slid over so she could have room to sit down.

"But I never said anything about–"

"Tell me, Lijin, how old were these kids when they were transported to the LEFP?" she cut me off. That's not what I thought she'd bring up.

"Oh, uh, eight, eight, and seven."

"So these kids were stripped from their homes at eight years or younger and placed in a mental asylum? Dear, of course they're gonna have trust issues. Just. Like. You." I hated it when she compared me to other people. "Lijin, do you remember how protective you were that day? When I met you?" I preferred not to. "That's how they're going to be towards each other. If someone is all you have, you ain't gonna let nobody take them from you."

I didn't respond. Of course they'd be territorial about each other.

They were all one another had.

"You've gotta remember all they've been through. Not to mention the fact that you don't know what happened that got them in there." She leaned forward to see my face clearer.

"...What do you have on the ritual?..." I finally asked, wanting to move the subject to something different. She smiled.

"All ready."

"...?! Really?!"

"Yes. I told Jaymon we'd do it tomorrow morning."

That was great news. "Oh, awesome!! So-so we can really fix her tomorrow?!" I exclaimed.

" 'Fix' is a strong word. I see nothing wrong with the girl." Mei stood and went to the door.

"Y-you know what I mean."

"Do I?"

"...Y-yeah. I don't mean *fix* her...I just mean...like...bring her back to normal," I tried to explain. Mei just nodded.

"Mmmh. I see. Well, watch your tongue. These kids are fragile." She grabbed the knob, then said, "I'll talk to them. The boys."

That confused me. "Not Xan?"

"Nope." She was so calm and confident with her answer, almost as if she'd been set on it for a while now. "You don't point out cracks to a shattered person. That just makes the pieces harder to pick up."

What does that mean? I wanted to ask. But I knew all too well what it meant. Pity is just insults after a while.

So Mei wasn't going to use pity or sympathy on the boys.

Not sure what her replacement was, but it worked. After about twenty minutes, both of them came back, grumbled an apology, and got over it. And when I pulled her out into the hallway and asked what she did, she just shrugged.

"A magician never shares her secret," was her response.

I scoffed at her reluctance, but let it go.

● ● ●

The rest of the afternoon was sluggish and lazy, which was honestly quite nice. Litz watched TV with Mei and I sat in my room with Jay and Rowan. Dinner was uneventful. Sam came down and prayed with us and then took her and Xan's plates up to her room. Xan never came down, but she at least ate because Samrinn brought back down two empty plates an hour later. We were all on the couches.

"How's Xan, honey?" Mei asked her. She meant her mental status.

Sam shrugged. "Okay, I guess. She's interesting."

Knowing how she rolled, I was immediately hit with possibilities.

"Hey, don't get any ideas!" I told her. Her face scrunched up.

"Ew, gross, no. I just meant that it's cool to listen to what she has to say," she informed. The boys stayed silent. Mei got up to go and wash the new dishes.

"So she's talking?" I asked. The girl nodded. "What's she said?" Jay was reading and his attention flicked away from the book to see her response. Rowan sat up straighter. Sam shrugged again without a word. "How do you not know?!"

"Calm down, Lijin. She just talked a little bit about what happened at lunch," she said.

"Which was?" Rowan questioned eagerly. "What'd she say?"

"Mmm...can't tell you." I'm not sure if she thought this was funny and worth joking about, but I was not gonna put up with tween sass.

"Samrinn, this is serious!" I told her.

"...I know," was her response. I was ticked off by then and on my last nerve. I opened my mouth to yell at her when she explained herself. "Xan told me that she didn't quite feel comfortable saying anything about it to you guys just yet, so I told her I wouldn't say anything." The male red-head seemed annoyed by the female red-head's explanation.

"So, basically, you're keeping secrets about her attacks because you two made a pinky promise?!" Rowan questioned. I could see Jay start to silently observe Samrish's movements as he grew more aggravated. Sam took a half step backwards in slight fear of the young escapee.

"No, she just—she—I mean I," she stammered, looking for words.

"Xan's not your place. If you've got anything that helps her, you're going to tell us!" He stood up. Litz plugged her ears across the room.

"Rowan, please calm down," Mei ushered as she popped back into the room.

"No! Xan's my friend and I don't plan on losing her!" he yelled, rather rudely, but I understood where he was coming from and I had expected the reaction. Though, I didn't know what to do. We weren't at the LEFP anymore, so I didn't feel that I had much authority in the situation. I was no longer a guard towards the children.

Suddenly, a wave of terror washed over me.

If Rowan—or any of them—got angry, I no longer had the right to hold them back, punish them, tell them off, or restrain them.

They're free, I reminded myself. *Not trapped behind prison walls, so...I can't do anything to restrain their actions.*

"I'm not keeping secrets from you!" Sam shot. "I'm just doing what I'm told!" She was starting to get upset, as well.

"Which is to keep secrets!!"

Jay's head popped with a stressed vein at his ruptured peace.

"Shut up..." he growled under his breath, but neither of them heard him. They continued spitting insults at each other. After a moment, Rivereay'd had enough. He slammed his book shut, jumping to his feet.

"Shut up!! Both of you!! Samrinn, stop fueling his fire!! Rowan, put a pin in it!!" he told them off. Sam looked shocked. Rowan calmed his tone, but stood his ground.

"Jay, seriously? You can't tell me you don't see anything wrong with this!" he said.

"I do," he replied with a stony aura. "But she's a kid and Xan's a 14-year-old with monstrous strength, enhanced emotions, and a teenage attitude. Not to mention she came from a prison! It's hard to accept, but if a person like that told you to shut your mouth, you're gonna zip it."

Rowan looked down in guilt and shame, tears in his eyes from the argument. I couldn't even guess at what was going through the poor kid's head. I wanted to say something, anything, that could help, but I couldn't find the right words.

Jay stepped closer to him so that he could lower his voice.

"Tomorrow morning, Rowan. You just gotta make it to tomorrow morning." I knew what he was talking about, but Rowan had not yet been informed. I had planned on telling him and talking it through with both boys when we went back upstairs. It was around 8:30 now, so I guess if they wanted to...

I noticed something at the top of the stairs. A person. They were silently watching everything go down. We locked eyes. Something sparked in me that hurt painfully, so I winced. When I opened my eyes again, Xan was gone.

No one else seemed to have noticed her. Jay went up the white-carpeted stairs after announcing that he'd be waiting for us in my room. Then he stopped at the top and spun back around.

"Oh, and Sam, tell Xan that I want my cat back," he said. She slowly nodded and he left my sight. Rowan sat down beside me, quiet.

My oh my...we're off to a great start, I moaned to myself.

~8:41~

I found myself sitting on my bed with one heathen in my desk chair and the other lying on his back on my floor with his current book held in the air, above his face. I sighed heavily, tired from the fourteen and a half miles I had walked (not including the river and everything after it) and the five hours of sleep I had gotten on the rocky floor of the cave.

"Rivereay, please put the book away," I groaned. He snapped his neck to the side to look at me.

"Why?"

"Because I need to talk to you guys about something."

Rowan swung his arms up in the air and immediately hit me with sarcasm. "Oh, great! More mom-speeches!"

"I don't give you mom-speeches!" I said to defend myself.

"...Mmm, yeah-huh."

"Whatever." Jay closed his story and sat up. I straightened my posture and Rowan lost his aloof composure. I had their attention.

"Okay, so, I think that we are going to do the ritual to reseal Xan tomorrow right after everybody wakes up. We have all the things necessary and it'll be fairly easy to set it all up. We are going to do it in this secret abandoned tunnel way thing that was found under the house. We need four candle holders, so I assumed you guys, me, and Meilynn. Sam and Litz will stay up here in Sam's room so that nothing happens to them. It'll keep them safe and out of the way. Uhh, I'd suggest keeping Rhekkun up here in the house, also. And–"

"Is it able to fail?" Rowan asked.

"...?" I was caught off-guard. "Well, uh, maybe? I mean, I-I think so. B-but it *shouldn't.*"

"What happens? You know, if the ritual somehow fails?"

"...Uh, well..." I dug through my memory, trying to recall the answer. The conversation between my mother and I about the ritual was fuzzy. I didn't really remember much of it. I mean, it *was* a long time ago. I would assume that the Terror would be released and the vessel killed, but I couldn't say that to them. Nor did it sound correct.

"I'm not sure," I admitted.

"Oh." He looked down in disappointment.

"So, Lijin," Jay said, "Mrs. Raq said that you need to draw the mark on the floor. You know what that looks like?" He meant Xan's hand.

It took me a second to respond. "Yes. I do, actually."

"...?" Jay's eyes widened.

"...?!" Rowan snapped his head up. "What?! Y-you do?! But she won't even show *us!*"

"Yeah. And to show *you*. Of all people," Jay agreed.

"Gee, thanks. And she never showed me." Shouldn't have said that. Jay leaned forward.

"...What?"

I tried to play it cool. "W-well, it just–I just looked it up one time. There's tons of stuff on search engines like *Google* and *Safari*." He just raised his eyebrows.

"Pictures of Xan's hand are on *Google*?"

"No. Uhm, remember she's not the first vessel." That got them off of me. Jay leaned back a bit, letting go of a bit of his aggression.

"Oh. Yeah. Right." He didn't sound exactly sold, but he let me be. "Anyway, doing this will be a *huge* accomplishment. We can save millions of people. I mean, this is the whole reason that we broke out, right? All that trouble won't be worth nothing," I exclaimed. Now, when Mei had told me to watch my tongue, she'd meant with things like that.

"..." That very noise was the sound that told me that I had messed up. I spun around to face the front of my room. In the doorway was a young girl in the standard prison uniform for the LEFP. Clutched in her arms was a small gray cat.

"X-Xan. What are you doing?" I questioned. Her head lowered.

"...Returning...Rhekkun...to Jay," she murmured.

"Oh, uh, thanks," Jaymon responded.

"...Yeah." But she made no move to give him the cat.

"Uh, Xan?" Rowan asked, sounding concerned. "You alright?"

She paused. "Once upon a time." Then she grimaced. She hadn't meant to say that. I could tell by her reaction.

"What does that–"

"I-I can't help but overhear...that everything we went through...was to save the stupid world. For four years...Lijin, you *watched* all that we had to go through. I thought that you had finally come to your senses, but...it wasn't even for us."

I was surprised at the fact that she would see it that way.

"Hold up, you don't understand. Doing this will save you, also. That's the main reason," I explained. Though, the girl didn't seem to believe me. Her violet eyes seemed at a loss of color as she stared at the floor. She loosened her grasp on the cat and she hopped down to perch at her feet. Xan clenched and unclenched her fists several times before responding.

"No it's not." Audible pain seeped out of her words.

What did Mist say to you? was all that came to mind.

"It really is, sweetie. We–Rowan, Jay, and I–like who you are. Something is letting Mist get closer to you and we can't let that happen. We're doing this because we truly long to save you." But my words fell upon deaf ears.

She ignored everything I was saying and stood for what she had first heard.

"All the people of this world ever do is chew us up and spit us back out! What part of that do you find worth saving?!" she asked.

"Xan, you aren't listening!" Jay told her. "We're doing it for *you*, not them!"

"Why in the world would I believe that?"

"...?" She seriously doubted our feelings towards her.

Rowan stood up. "Because it's the truth!" he pleaded. But she ignored his cries. She wasn't listening. She was hurt too deeply.

"I don't know what this 'ritual' thing is or why I wasn't informed of it, but I'm glad that's all that this was for. Now I have no reason to stay here. With you guys." She shook her head in disbelief then took a step backwards. I hopped to my feet and reached out my hand in a pathetic attempt of begging her to hear me. But she had left the room before the girl's name had even fully left my mouth.

I fell to my bed, head in hands. Across the room from me, Rowan slowly lowered his body back into the chair.

"Rhekkun, c'mere, girl," Jaymon whispered to the smokey gray cat that still sat in the doorway. She looked back and forth between him and the direction that Xan had run off in, indecisive. Then she made a '*merow*' sound and scurried off to find the girl. Jay exhaled heavily.

"That could've gone better," Rowan muttered after a moment.

"Not likely." *Not again.* I turned my head to find Mei standing at my door. Rowan and Jay both looked up to meet her gaze, as well.

"What does that mean?" I dared to ask.

"It seems mentally impossible for that girl to process anything that has to do with receiving love or kindness." I was pretty much *done* with the lectures. I was tired. And hurting.

"Just stop putting on the 'old-and-wise' act and actually talk to me!!" I snapped unintentionally. Though, she didn't seem surprised by that.

"Fine. Stop acting like a total wuss and open your eyes to the fact that that girl has been alone for so long that she physically refuses to accept that anyone could ever love her! Imagine being fourteen with her problems–!"

"Her problems?!" I yelled, standing back up. "I watched her first problem unfold!!" The boys were puzzled by that, but I yelled at them and turned it down before they could even ask. "Three months, Mei! Remember that?! Three months."

"Yes. And you were so broken. Now imagine fifteen years. You can feel. You can guess. You can sympathize. But you will never know. Her emotions run too deep."

I paused, catching my breath and thinking that over.

"Sorry for yelling at you, dear. I'm gonna go tell the girls goodnight. Boys, Lijin's tired. Why don't you guys go ahead and wash up and go to sleep. Tomorrow's big. You'll need a lot of rest to be ready for it," Mei said. They left without question.

I stared at the floor, embarrassed at my outrage.

"Lijin." I didn't look up. "Sleep well." She walked over and kissed my forehead. "She's here, sweetheart," was all she said before she walked out and shut the door behind her.

Yeah...Sh-she's here...

And more messed up than I was on the day I lost everything.

And I was almost to the point where I couldn't be fixed.

Could she?

suicide
many times have i considered this
and found it to be a way out
after a certain amount of lonely
i decided this to be a new route
the temptation is like the one of
dying of thirst in front of a water spout
i've gotten close to taking up this offer
but then a voice in my head shouts,

really? death?
you think they'll notice you're gone?
really, all you're doing
is sacrificing a useless pawn

so i gave it some thought
and though it filled my heart with sorrow,
i found myself living out
yet another tomorrow

–PRISONER JOURNAL OF
SUBJECT 3029

twenty-second 5742

It was the same dream. I woke up at the same point. I was hot, sweaty, and panting from the nightmare. I sat up, trying to catch my breath. For a moment, I couldn't remember where I was. My head slowly turned and I scanned the room. It was a fairly decent sized room with pale walls that were lit by the soft moonlight pouring in from the window. A small bed-side table held a lamp that was shut off since it was the middle of the night. My—Taku's—bag was in the far corner on an egg shaped seat. This was the interior of one of Meilynn Teraki's spare rooms.

I was hit with the fogginess of sleep and my body naturally attempted to slump back down. But I stayed upright, feeling like something was off. In my hand, as usual, was the small red and yellow blanket that I had owned since my childhood. I felt childish about being old enough to drive a car and still sleeping with a baby blanket, but it gave me security.

I unraveled it from my fingers and tossed off the heavy covers. I swung my legs over the side of the bed and hopped to the ground.

The house was silent besides the AC. I took precautions, stepping as quietly and lightly as I could, but Meilynn's house did not sway and echo like the LEFP did. It was weird. I wasn't used to it.

I had planned to stalk out the kitchen and just get, like, water or something, but my plans quickly changed when I reached the living room. For I was not the only one up.

Sitting in the windowsill was a girl. Her hair was completely down and messy as though she had been asleep up until now. Her eyes were just barely visible and they reflected the neighborhood outside. Her left hand was hidden behind her body while her right was wound loosely around her knees. The starlight bounced off of her pale skin, seemingly making her shine. I couldn't move. It was such a pretty sight.

I didn't think that she had noticed me until she spoke.

"It's not nice to stare, Rowan," Xan whispered. I flushed red and looked down at my feet.

"Sorry," I apologized. She turned to face me. She was wearing a short sleeved T-shirt with a white base with some random anime character on it, gray shorts, and tall socks. It was an outfit that had been provided by Sam. Xan was so small that Samrinn's clothes actually fit her quite nicely. Jay and I had just gone to sleep in our pants and surprisingly snug fitting tank tops that belonged to Lijin. It was, honestly, really nice to wear something other than our uniforms.

I could feel her staring at me, so I lifted my head back up to meet her gaze.

"...?" It startled me at how much pain was visible deep in her violet eyes. It had become so much easier to tell what Xan was thinking ever since her emotions got enhanced. But it hurt to realize that she was in pain *all the time*. For the longest time, she had just hidden it.

"You alright?" I asked, concern highly audible in my voice. Her mouth opened. Then shut. Her head slightly shook like she was wisping away a thought.

"Y-yeah. I'm just...tired," she responded. I didn't buy it.

"Tired? Then why are you up?"

She turned back to the window. "Not necessarily in that sense. What are you doing up?"

"Thirsty." In all technicality, I wasn't lying.

"*Dipsasménos. Ti dikaiología.*"

"...?!" I couldn't understand what it said, but I knew what said it. And that was enough to freak me out. While I panicked, Xan stayed calm. Her face just churned in a mixture of sorrow and annoyance.

"Leave me alone," she muttered.

"W-what did it say?" I dared to ask.

"He," she corrected. "He's male. And his name is Kakó. And he was making fun of your excuses." So she could understand it–I mean, him–while no one on the outside could. When what I heard was Greek, she heard the same thing, but as if it was in English. That wasn't creepy.

"Oh. Heh...okay." I rubbed my neck, not sure what to say.

After about a minute of awkward silence, Xan spoke.

"I just–...I still feel locked up." That's not what I had expected to hear. And it confused me.

"But, Xan, we escaped the LEFP. We're not in there anymore."

"That's not what I mean. I feel like I'm back to being trapped in my little room. My...parents...too scared of me to come in. I wasn't allowed to go outside; to make human contact. To show my face."

"But you have free reign of the house. And I'd bet that Mei would let you outside if you asked," I told her. The massive tree waved in the breeze outside.

"We're escapees, Rowan. There are guards and police everywhere, searching for us. In the last fifteen minutes, I've seen seven cop cars go by. We're on the run. Who's to say that someone won't turn us in for prize money the moment they recognize our faces? They've probably already sent out alerts and we've most likely been on the NEWS several times. We can't go outside. I'm surprised that no one saw us come in here. We aren't safe." I-I hadn't viewed it in that way.

"What did...Kakó say to you earlier?" I asked, changing the subject. She looked at me, her eyes gazing into mine. Her mouth opened as if she was going to tell me, but she shut it just as quickly and turned away.

"I'm not ready to say anything," she admitted. I didn't mean to get mad at her. She was going through a lot and, as her friend, I should have had the patience to wait for her. But I was still upset over the whole Sam thing.

"Well then how come you told Sam?! You haven't lived with her for seven years! She hasn't watched you break down! She wasn't there for you when reality hit you harder than other days! She doesn't know you like Jay and I do. So how come she gets to know, but we don't?"

That hit her hard.

"I never told Sam, Rowan." She sounded so hurt.

"...?...W-what?"

"I never told her," she repeated. "I just gave her a basic outline. Kakó gave me info from my past that I didn't know and it had really shocked me. That's all I told her."

"So I...at her...for no..." My words were staggered and my thoughts incomplete. But somehow, she knew what I meant.

"Yeah, you went off on her for no reason."

"...Could you hear?"

"Yes. I was at the top of the stairs."

"Oh." I hadn't known that. Had I, and I wouldn't have done things the way I had. But the way she'd put it had just made me feel so lied to. I hated being lied to. Everyone did.

That's why I hated not knowing what was *truly* going on with Xan. I couldn't help fix what I didn't know.

"Rowan?" Xan asked.

"Yeah?" I responded.

"What's this 'ritual' thing? And how come I hadn't been informed of it until last night?" Oh yeah. No one had told her.

"Well, in a nutshell, it will reseal Mist back inside of you so that you don't have your attacks anymore and we don't run the risk of him escaping."

"Oh, yeah. That conversation."

"...I-it's not what you think. It really is for you."

"...You should go back to sleep," was her reply.

"You did this at the cave, too. Why don't you trust me enough to let me help you?"

"I-I do trust you, it's just..." She stopped and took a deep breath, making a decision. "Rowan, my parents died a long time ago."

I felt my eyes go wide. "...? Wh-what?"

"My mother died giving birth and my father was killed because I was left in his hands. My 'parents' now aren't my real ones. I'm adopted. That's what Kakó told me. I'm trying to process it. The cave was a whole 'nother story."

There. Now I knew. And yet, I didn't feel any better.

I couldn't answer. I just stood there, flabbergasted.

"...It's two in the morning. You should go back to bed," Xan repeated.

I shut my eyes and squeezed them so tight that my face hurt.

"I want to help you..." I told her.

"Rowan, after the ritual, you won't have to pretend to accept me. You can go on your way." I was starting to get upset with her reluctance.

"Xan, stop it! I don't *pretend* anything. Nothing will change after tomorrow."

"I'm a capsule for a Terror. Have you forgotten?"

"Quit! You don't listen anymore! You're losing your character." I was trying my hardest to keep my voice down since everyone was asleep upstairs, but it was getting tricky. I was so angry. Xan's features became scary and her eyes seemed to lose their bright color.

"No. I'm adapting to my new one."

"...?!" It felt like the wind had been knocked out of me and yet, I continued standing and my breathing did not rupture. Was I really losing the Xan I cherished? Would she ever go back to normal? What if she hated me after this fight and I lost her for good?

"Y-you don't have to change your character," I murmured, a desperate tone to my voice.

"Oh, but I do. I'm not going to let him eat me, Rowan. If I'm going down, I'm going down fighting," Xan responded.

"But it's not fighting…"

"Then what is it, hmm? Tell me."

I tried to choose my words carefully, but still really could have done much better. "Pardon my answer, but you're turning yourself into the monster that you're rumored to be."

"…?" I knew she'd internalize it, but it was all I'd had to say.

"Xan, my brother *killed* himself at the *sight* of me. I know what it's like to feel like a monster. It hurts. But…*adapting to it*…is a *whole* different ball game."

She lifted her left hand and rotated it ever so slowly in front of her face to get a good picture of the black glove and blue lines. Her eyes shook with a welling emotion that I couldn't quite identify.

"That thing doesn't define you. What you do with it does," I told her.

Her legs were quickly thrown off the windowsill and she leapt into a step towards me with her hand outstretched. She moved so fast.

"Rowan, I–"

That's where I went wrong. My body, without my permission, subconsciously made me take a step away from her. It was an instinct. One that I immediately regretted having. Xan instantly froze. The look of pain on her face violently shook me to my core. I noticed that my heart was racing. I threw my hands out in front of me to try and explain.

"I-I-I, I didn't, I mean, I-I wasn't supposed to s-step back. Y-you, you just startled me! And I-" I stammered helplessly.

"Rowan...are you...scared of me?" Xan asked.

"N-no! Trust me, Xan, I just—" She held up her hand and shook her head sadly.

"You know I have good hearing. I always have. That's why the bell always hurt me so much. But now, with all of my senses enhanced, I hear so much more. I hear your pulse. And it hurts me to figure out that you guys are *terrified* of me and lie a *lot*. My "parents" are scared of me. The world is scared of me. Hell, I'm scared of myself. It was kind of nice having the reassurance of my best friends."

She walked over to me and, while I shut my eyes in an internal protective stance, stopped to whisper in my ear.

"But I guess that was never there."

Then she walked upstairs and left me.

It took me a second to move, but when I did, I was instantly furious and holding back tears. I brought my hands to my face and dug my nails into my skin as I covered my eyes.

"Damn it...!" I dug my nails deeper and then thrust my hands down. "Damn it, damn it!!"

The young man who has stolen my next project turns out to be more special than he lets on. Birth name: Lijin N. Kozvick, current name: Lijin N. Teraki. For 6 years, he was the only legal son of Cooper R., the "one and only legend". Ugh. Exaggeration, much? But Cooper's wife on the other hand...

He may be more of a prize than I had thought...

G. Qinglee

–EXPERIMENT JOURNAL OF

SERGEANT 0001

twenty-third   3029

"Xan. Xan. Xan! Wake up!"

I snapped open my eyes, startled, and yanked my body away from the intruder. I hit the wall with my back and then the ceiling with my head. Then everything came into focus. Samrinn–Lijin's little sister–was standing on top of her bed with her hands on the dark wooden railing of the top bunk. Her long hair was in a loose braid with countless fly-aways. She was wearing an oversized T-shirt and shorts that were barely visible. I glanced down. Same.

I sat back down, grimacing at the pain in the top of my head. "Ouch," I complained. Sam giggled. I rubbed the fogginess of sleep out of my eyes. Memory hit me quickly. My stomach tightened. Last night was my fight with Rowan. What would happen if he held all of that against me? What would I do?

"Uh, you alright?" Sam asked. I was so tired of those words.

"Yes. I'm fine. Now why'd you wake me up?"

"Because Mom told me to." She smiled innocently. I rubbed my eyes again. This was my second morning without the bell. Yesterday, I woke up naturally. It was weird to be woken up by a person.

"Okay, well, what time is it?"

"6:30," Sam responded immediately. That shocked me.

"Pft, s-s-six thirty?! Don't you people sleep?!" The LEFP's bell rang at 7:00 and yesterday was different since I had been filled with the adrenaline of escaping.

Samrinn laughed. "Mom wanted to do the ritual now. Plus, everyone else is already up." Great. The kid knew about the ritual and I didn't. I sighed to myself and then crawled across the bed to its ladder. I climbed down it and Sam jumped down to the floor beside me. She skipped over to her closet and flung the doors open.

"Alrighty, then! What are we wearing? Oh, uh, yeah. You can wear some of my clothes again if you'd like to," she offered.

"Uh, well..." I said, still in indecision of her kindness. "How about...–" Then I realized how big this was. If I had processed Rowan's brief explanation correctly, then this would reseal Kakó. No more attacks. No more fits. No more weird visions. No more horrifying thoughts. No more outbursts. I'd be normal again. And though I got stares and heard rumors and got treated like crap by some of the guards, the normalist I have ever felt was with Rowan and Jay at the LEFP.

I turned to look at the black bag that was hanging at the top of the ladder.

"Actually...I had a different outfit in mind."

• • •

I came down the stairs in an off-white button-up shirt with the top button left open, soft black pants, no shoes or socks, and a small fingerless glove that reached just a little ways past my wrist. My hair was left down besides a large braid on the left side of my head. My outfit wasn't completely clean since it was the same one that I had just cleaned in the stream, but it did the trick.

The first to spot me was Lijin.

"You're wearing your uniform?" he questioned with a smile on his face. Everyone turned at the indication that someone had come downstairs. Rowan's eyes lit up when he saw me, but then the spark quickly vanished and he looked down.

"Yeah," I replied. "I started in my uniform, why shouldn't I end in it?"

He shrugged. "Good enough."

Samrinn ran over to him and Mei, and they chatted lustily. Litz was no- where to be seen. I walked over to Rowan. He was wearing his pants and a dark blue T-shirt. I could still see the bandages that spiraled around his shoulder from where he had been shot.

"H-hey, Rowan."

"H-hi." He seemed surprised that I would speak to him. I jumped right into what I wanted to say.

"Listen, about last night, I-I didn't really mean that. Well, I mean, I-I did, I wasn't lying. But it–I didn't really feel that...strongly towards it. You know? It just, with the whole...emotion stuff, it just comes out more...intense than...–I'm not making any sense." I sighed, taking a deep breath, and retried. "Listen, I just...I'm sorry. It's really hard to get used to–and I know that's not a real excuse, but...I want to apologize to you for the way I took it."

He just stood there for a moment. It started to make me anxious, like he might reject my apology. We hadn't even fought that bad, but my last words made it sound like I thought our friendship was fake. Which I didn't! Well...if I thought about it...–Wait no! I-I trusted the bond that we shared!

When his mouth *finally* opened, Jay stepped in and cut him off, hands stuffed in his pockets.

"I'm just gonna saunter over here, then. Oh, hey guys! Didn't see ya there; now are you two done squabbling, yet?" His outfit was identical to Rowan's except for the fact that his shirt was dark red. I gave a quick pleading glance to Rowan, wanting him to be the one to answer Jay's question.

Relief flooded through me when he gave off an aloof smile and responded with, "I'm ready to be." I grinned. Then, I decided to stick out my right fist. Both of them just stared at it.

"Oh, come on. I know you remember," I told them.

"I-it's been like three years," Rowan reminded me. I knew that. Jay rolled his eyes and connected his right fist to mine. Next was Rowan. Leaving our right hands where they were, we hit our left ones together vertically, overtop of the original bump. We swung our top hands down, up, left, right, then back to their starting position. Then we withdrew them, rotated them ninety degrees, bumped them together, and flung them out. We erupted with laughter as we dropped both hands to our sides.

Only a little while after joining the LEFP had my parents' abandonment really hit me. My guard before Lijin was...well...sort of abusive. He had told me, when I cried, that if I couldn't live with it, then he'd just kill me himself. I never cried in front of him again. Because I was so freaking scared to. I had held it all in until, one day, randomly, while we were in Rowan's room, I lost it. I had been either eight or nine years old, so I hadn't really figured out how to cope with the pain.

If I remember correctly, I sobbed my heart out for about ten minutes before Taku opened the door, concerned and deeply annoyed. Rowan and Jay had yelled at him like there was no tomorrow. Once I had finally calmed down, Rowan taught us this handshake.

"*It's like an oath,*" he'd told us.

"*An...oath?*"

"*Yeah! We'll go through everything together. We've got your back.*" I could still remember the overwhelming emotion that had filled me with.

"*Exactly,*" Jay'd agreed.

I had taken a deep breath. "*And I got yours.*"

We hadn't done the handshake in a while, but that moment was engraved in our hearts. It was the true beginning of our friendship. It was when it had been set in stone for the rest of our lives that we would do all of this stupid crap as a group. Together.

Lijin's voice brought me back to the present. "Okay. Are we ready?" I nodded. "Alrighty. Let's go." He sent Sam upstairs and then led us through the house to a door that was located in a closet behind *another* door. It was dark and, after a split second of my eyes adjusting, I realized that it was a bunch of creepy stone stairs that seemingly never ended as you walked down to the underworld. I turned to Lijin.

"What the heck is this?!" He shrugged, clicking on a flashlight.

"It was here when Mei moved in."

"This is where corpses are stored," Rowan muttered.

"Just come on." He pointed the flashlight at the stairs and started down them. Mei walked behind us, taking up the rear with a flashlight of her own. My heart started racing more and more the longer we walked for. I was getting scared, nervous. I had the natural instinct to hold the hands of my friends for comfort. Neither of them were weird about it, so I did it all the time. But something felt different. Right now, I held back. I was suddenly very conscious of the ugly mark that my glove covered. No human being deserved to be stabbed by the thorns of my left hand. Only I should endure that.

The stairs went on for what felt like forever. It was never going to end! I found myself opening my mouth to complain when the ground finally came into view. I gasped. It was huge!! *What in the world?!* The floor had to have been around 800 square feet in area, maybe larger. There was a large gap after that with tracks running at the bottom. That hole extended out of view both ways, left and right. It took me a second to realize that it was a subway station since I'd never seen one.

"Whoa," was all I could say. Nobody had quite a reaction because they still couldn't see. Rowan and Jay just looked confused.

"Uh, Lijin? Where's, like, the candles?" Rowan asked.

"In your corners," Meilynn told him like it was obvious. She crossed her fingers in an irregular way and the area lit up slightly with a pale blue light. About 100 feet to the right of me was an orangish-red candle. 100 feet in the opposite direction was the same candle just in green. 100 feet in front of that was a yellow one. And then 100 feet to the side from *that one* was a black one. The four candles formed a perfect square. In the exact center was a purple one. Most likely for me.

"Well, uh, where's the seal that was supposed to be drawn on the ground?" Jaymon questioned as he looked the area up and down in awe.

"It's there," Lijin responded. Jay's gaze flicked around.

"No it's not."

"Yes, it is. You just can't see it."

"Well then, who can?"

"The Terror."

I looked around.

"There's nothing there," I announced. Teraki started making his way towards the yellow candle.

"You don't have Kakó's eye."

"...?" The reaction was mainly in response to his quick and casual reply about the 2nd Great Terror. It never dawned on me that he said 'eye' as in one.

Or that he used Kakó's name.

Mei walked over to the green candle on my left, telling the boys that one of them needed to go to each of the leftover candles. Without replies, they both tapped my shoulder in turn and Rowan went for the black while Jay picked up the orange. In seconds, every candle had a holder.

"Now, Xan, sweetie, you need to go and sit with the purple one," Mei called out to me. I swallowed, then nervously walked over. After hesitating for a split second, I bent down to grab it.

"Wait!!" Lijin yelled. He startled me and I shot away from the candle. He set down his and ran up to me, pulling something out of his pocket. "Sorry. We just forgot something." He laughed it off, but I was furious that he had made me feel like I had done something wrong, my cheeks burning.

He opened up the thing in his hands, dipped his pointer finger in, and then tried to touch my forehead. I pulled away in shock.

"Hey, whoa! What are you doing?!"

"Oh, calm down," he said.

"What is that?!" I demanded.

"Xan, it's just water."

"So, do you always carry a weird tiny container of water on you?"

He chuckled. "You could say that. But it's *special* water."

I waved my arms around exaggeratively. "Oh, great. Holy water. Hurray. Why are you baptizing me?"

"Xan, I...I put a ragitou on it. It's part of the ritual." I wasn't quite sure what a ragitou was, but if it was part of the ritual, then it was deemed necessary. Lijin knew more than I did here, so I guess I had to trust his judgment.

"...Oh." I leaned forward a bit so that he could reach me. Lijin re-dipped his finger in the ragitou-ified water. Then he placed the tip of his finger a little bit above the center of my forehead and drug it downward. The motion felt weirdly familiar. He stopped for a second, not lifting his finger. It took me a moment to realize that it was shaking.

"You alright?" I asked. He shook his head slightly, clearing something. His finger stilled and then left my head.

"Yeah."

He drug his finger horizontally through the middle of the first line, forming a cross. He wiped his finger on his shirt and then closed the weird container that held the rest of the water and shoved it in his pocket.

"Okay. All set. Now, I don't know how much it'll hurt or even if it'll hurt at all. But once we start, we can't stop. Got it? Are you ready?"

I thought about it, hesitant. Then I nodded, my decision made. "Yes. I am."

"Okay," Lijin repeated. He took a deep breath in and exhaled slowly. He must've been about as nervous as I was. "Let's do this, then, kiddo." He scurried back over to his candle.

The water did not run down my nose, but instead soaked into my skin. I crouched down, ready to touch the candle. I gazed around the square at everyone else. Rowan and Jay both smiled when they met my eyes. That filled me with a little bit of confidence. And no matter how small, it was there. I could totally do this. Right?

But I was not prepared for the little shock that I was in for.

Right when my fingertips reached the wax, I was hit with blaring pain. My head was jolted back at an irregular angle and I lost sight of the ritual space. Then I got a vision.

It was the same vision as the one from lunch. Except, this time, I only saw two people. The boy with the green eyes and the girl with the white eyes. But, the girl's left eye was bleeding at a ferocious rate. My eye throbbed watching her. The boy lifted his right arm and swung it downward. And then I was released back into my world.

I fell backward, but I didn't pass out. I was gasping for air.

"Xan?!" I couldn't tell who said it.

Something hot rolled down from my nose. I reached up and touched it to find that it was bleeding. My head and arm both ached.

"Kakó, what was that?!" I murmured.

"*I don't know. Maybe a reaction to the candle?*" he said.

"That was not a reaction to the stupid candle!"

"*You never know.*"

"Kakó!"

"*Listen, RJ, I don't know what that was. I didn't do it. Really.*" I tightened my jaw. Something was wrong.

"Xan, are you alright? We can wait if we need to! It's okay! We haven't started yet!" Lijin called out to me. But I turned his offer down.

"No," I said, getting to my feet. I picked up the candle hesitantly, but nothing happened. I sat down criss-crossed and held it in my lap. "Okay, well, here goes nothing."

With my words, Rowan, Jay, Lijin, and Mei started chanting some Greek crap that I didn't pay attention to. Their four candles lit one by one. Wind picked up. Remember, we were underground. Yeah, that makes sense. I wiped my nose with the back of my hand, and then closed my eyes. My candle lit.

My arm burst into agony, but I only grimaced. I did not move.

Then there was a loud 'POP' behind my eyes. Everything flashed white. I screamed, but it caught in my throat and no sound came out. I could hear my candle whip out and the flame disperse into floating sparks. Something burst, but I couldn't tell what. Everything hurt and I couldn't see.

"XAN!!"

"XAN!"

"XANDRALIN!!"

"XAN?!"

"*RJ!!*"

I lost sense of everything. The lights went out. My body fell. The candle in my hands slipped away and broke. My heart gave off its last dying beat, and then shut down.

(TO BE CONTINUED, THE ELEMENTAL WARS: MIST)

THE MUCH NEEDED

* Character Index *

~MAIN CHARACTERS:

~IMPORTANT CHARACTERS:

~VILLAINS:

~SIBLINGS:

Samrinn Teraki … … … (sam-rin) (ter-rock-ee) … … … '**' … … … Lijin's younger sister

Litz Teraki … … … (lits) (ter-rock-ee) … … … '**' … … … Lijin's other younger sister

Daniel Samrish … … … (dan-yull) (sam-rish) … … … '**' … … … Rowan's elder brother

Alice Rivereay … … … (al-iss) (riv-ear-A) … … … '**' … … … Jay's younger sister

Ethaniel Teraki … … … (E-th-an-yull) (ter-rock-ee) … … … '**' … … … Lijin's elder brother

~GUARDS:

Taku Cazven … … … (tock-oo) (cazz-ven) … … … 7512 … … … Rowan's personal guard

Ivan Gaal … … … (eye-van) (gull) … … … 11463 … … … Jay's personal guard

Innkuro Whosivitch … … … (in-ker-O) (who-suh-vitch) … … … 9921 … … … a guard

Galry Righteous … … … (gull-ree) (ruh-eye-chus) … … … 7007 … … … a service guard

Beighley Nance … … … (bay-lee) (nan-ss) … … … 8296 … … … the LEFP's nurse

Troy Macendail … … … (t-roy) (mac-en-dale) … … …10893 … … … one of the pursuers; guard

Larisa O'rell … … … (la-riss-uh) (oh-rell) … … … 12214 … … … the other pursuer; a guard

author's notes Mist

First things first, thank you so much for reading the Elemental Wars: Mist! The book you're holding right now in your hands was my very first book to ever be written and completed and it's become the center of my life. This book was started back in March of 2022 when I was only eleven years old. Now, hear me out, I was pretty young–and I still am–so you might have to be patient with me. Just a little teensy bit. My writing isn't going to be the best you've ever seen and there's always going to be room for me to improve, but that's the best part! I get to push myself to be better with every book I make.

I've been telling stories my whole life and writing them since I was around five or six. Fantasy has always been my way of escaping reality and Bludriss is my very own realm. I created Xan and her friends to help me find myself. Xan herself was based on my own personality. I made her struggle with a lot of unspoken problems to help give voice to my own. And it's one of the most therapeutic things I've ever experienced.

I have had so many people help me on this crazy ride. I've had my readers, my listeners, my editors, my suggesters, my supporters, and my contributors. My dream has always been to make a world where everything is magical. Where everyone has a story that can unfold in beautifully messy pages. And that's exactly the goal that I have achieved.

With the help of everyone around me, I've been able to create this world and make my dream a reality. A special shoutout to my cousin and cover artist, Lindsey, my mom, Jackie, my dad, Steven, my little brother, Lucas, my aunts, Julie and Pam, my grandmas, Doris and Kay, my little cousin/soul-sister, Rylee Shea, my best friends, Kenna, Noah, Rialynn, Julie, Evelyn, Caleb B, Ethan, Caleb W, Naomi, Arabelle, and Isabelle, my eighth grade ELA and Writing Club teacher Mrs. Nungester, and anyone else who guided me on this stupidly awesome journey. Oh, and how could I forget? Thank you, as a reader, for helping me, as well.

I have in some way or another spiraled a lot of dark truths about today's generation throughout the entirety of either this book or the rest of the series. Over time, my characters deal with things as in depression, suicide, eating disorders, loneliness, drugs, alcohol, sexual assault, ADHD, anxiety, murder, and of course (though I came at it with more of a literal approach) inner demons.

I've faced a lot throughout middle school and it all has made me contemplate my self worth. And nobody knows because of how I have coped with it. I latched on to the people around me and let them know that they were not alone with whatever crap they were going through. I don't know how, but this helped. I can't really put it into words, but it kinda saved me.

Being able to save my friends. It kept me there. It gave me a purpose. And knowing that they were OK meant that, hey, maybe I'll be OK too.

Soooo, to try and help explain this, I took four people with entirely different backgrounds and placed them all in the same situation where they have to relive what they've been through to save someone they love. The chapters alternate between perspectives so that the reader always knows more than anyone else does. They get to watch as each grieving character places on a smile and writhes inside as they compare what they had done to what they (think they) could have done. As each of them shrink and resort to suffering on their own, truths begin to unfold and they all learn that everyone is going through something similar. They learn that they are not alone. Because of this, they latch on to their friends and start to realize that just because they aren't whole, doesn't mean they have to be considered broken.

Jay, Rowan, Xan, and Lijin are all hard on themselves. They're all silently blaming themselves for a past that no one yet knows about. And it starts to kill them when Xan's life is placed in danger. So they have to try to figure out how to live with what has happened in order to be strong enough to fight off whatever is coming for them.

My books aren't about finding the light in the darkness. I know that for me, sometimes that just seemed way too hard. So instead, they're about finding the strength and motivation to get up off your sorry ass and look. You don't have to find it immediately. You don't even have to move towards it. Just look. And I promise, it'll be worth your while. Even if you don't see it immediately, doesn't mean it isn't there.

I know what it's like to feel like you're lost in the dark and nobody really sees you. I do. I really do. Each of my characters do too. All of them. Even the happy ones. Because even though they lost almost everything in the past, they've found each other to fight for. They got up, looked around, and found other people lost in that tunnel with them.

Xan, a demon vessel, Rowan, the boy who drowned his parents, Jaymon, who won't even talk about what happened to cause his sister to die, and Lijin, whose parents died in front of him three times. They're all outcasts. Like you and me.

But they haven't given up, now, have they?

Even if the ritual...oh yeah. The ritual. You still don't know what happened. I bet you *want* to know what happened, don't 'cha? Well, then, I guess I better wrap this up so that you can get on over to the next book!

Once again, thank you so so so much for reading this and I hope to be able to continue this magical action series and see you in book two, the Elemental Wars: Earth!

Kiss, kiss, kiss~~Hug, hug, hug

Liv Elizabeth Clark

(May 18, 2024)

Mist

www.ingramcontent.com/pod-product-compliance
Lightning Source LLC
Chambersburg PA
CBHW021505240626
47154CB00002B/509